MONA LISA SMILED A LITTLE

Mona Lisa Smiled a Little

A NOVEL

Rachel Wyatt

OOLICHAN BOOKS
LANTZVILLE, BRITISH COLUMBIA, CANADA
1999

Canadian Cataloguing in Publication Data

Wyatt, Rachel, 1929-
  Mona Lisa smiled a little

ISBN 0-88982-180-1 (bound) — ISBN 0-88982-176-3 (pbk.)
  I. Title.
PS8595.Y3M66 1999   C813'.54 C99-910193-5
PR9199.3.W88M66 1999

We gratefully acknowledge the support of the Canada Council for the Arts for our publishing program.

THE CANADA COUNCIL | LE CONSEIL DES ARTS
FOR THE ARTS | DU CANADA
SINCE 1957 | DEPUIS 1957

Grateful acknowledgement is also made to the BC Ministry of Tourism, Small Business and Culture for their financial support.

We acknowledge the financial support of the Government of Canada through the Book Publishing Industry Development Program for our publishing activities.

Canadä

Published by
Oolichan Books
P.O. Box 10, Lantzville
British Columbia, Canada
V0R 2H0

Printed in Canada by
Morriss Printing Company Ltd.
Victoria, British Columbi:

To my family with love

Acknowledgements

The author would like to thank the Canada Council for its generous support, Ursula Vaira and Ron Smith for their encouragement and careful editing, and Alan for always being there.

"The Hobby" first appeared in *Quarry*.

"The Hobby," "Becoming Chinese," and "Sometimes I Look at Younger Men" were published in slightly different form in *The Day Marlene Dietrich Died* (Oolichan 1996).

The Hobby

Almeida knew that other women's husbands had innocent hobbies. She had met men in bars and in theatres
and occasionally on horseback who talked of electric
trains, of rare stamps or of birdsong. One day when she
was standing up to her hips in water, the man beside her
asked if she would like to buy an entire box full of match-
box covers. She loved him at once for his ordinariness,
but just then a fish tugged at his line and pulled him
farther out into the river.

It was not that Joe had maliciously chosen to fill the
house with imitations of her, it simply seemed beyond
his power to stop. The counsellor had said, "A retired
man needs a hobby," as if she, Almeida, was the villain
in this piece. For a while she had accepted that role. She
had swept and tidied where she could and set meals down
on stairs and in corners and tried to tell him that her

hair had never looked like that. And then, when there seemed to be no way of getting his attention, she had decided to "distance herself from the problem."

So he had his hobby, she had hers. She bought tickets. He bought wood. She bought maps. He bought new chisels. She moved around the country and wrote postcards to him and to the children from far away. She took photographs and stood up in small boats to see better views and heard her own voice talking too loudly to strangers. He stayed at home and carved her features out of maple and gave her the fifties hairdo of a Dietrich, the proud look of a beautiful woman.

Last month, out there in the mountains, she had begun to think that she was wasting too much time on scenery. She had to stop reaching out to it and endowing it with magic. She had allowed rocks and waterfalls to offer her lifelines. She had lived by scenery, as though it was her own soul but external. And now it was time to walk backwards away from all that grandeur and become a person who asked the advice of others.

The fact that Joe had been right about the west was not in his favour. It only meant that he had been in that place in his youth, without her, singing perhaps, enjoying himself, his hands still. And that he had, somewhere, underneath all those heads, some pictures of his own.

"Be patient," the counsellor had said to her and had gone on to explain the sudden-peace syndrome. Men and women of Joe's age, brought up to fight, ready, even eager to go over there and kill or be killed, had been stopped by the surrender of the enemy. Peace had broken out and side-lined them. Allowances had to be made. But that was nearly fifty years ago, Almeida had replied, and surely time had cured them of their belligerence.

She sat in the living room across from Jean and dipped a hard oatmeal cookie into her tea. Bits were left floating in the cup. It was not attractive.

"You've been back two days," Jean said.

"Do I have to keep going away?"

"Have you confronted him?"

"Confront," they said. "Be aggressive. Go to assertiveness class. It's your house too." She had heard those words often. She had heard irritation in the voices which spoke the words out loud. Seen anger on the faces of her daughters. But all of it was easy to say. When she heard them saying it, she felt homesick for canyons and crevasses and the very edge of the land.

So she said, "I've come back to tell him, to offer him love, to consider, I think, starting over."

Jean said, "He must notice when you're not there."

"Half the house is mine."

"But he takes up all of it. You should have half, Almeida. You paid for half."

That too was easy to say when halves were so hard to define. What if, in each room, she owned the upper half where the air was better? Maybe the rooms could be divided in a zigzag way allowing her certain uncluttered parts. Or perhaps the outer shell of the house was all hers, the brick walls, the red-tiled roof, the chimney; and the inner space all his.

"Or I might move away for good."

"Some people wonder why you haven't. Why haven't you?"

Even the best of the mountains had given Almeida no answer to that. Last Wednesday, standing on the shore of the Pacific, she saw that she could go no further unless she seriously considered flight. And so she had returned home to confront, to be assertive, to make up her mind.

She gritted her teeth and moved on to the second reason for her visit. Jean had been friend and neighbour for years. But exasperation and age had come between them. And a certain amount of envy. After all, she could, she did, travel at certain times for weeks, cheaply and by bus but still it was travel, it was getting away. Jean stayed at home and her home was at least three quarters hers. Her thirty-year-old son stayed in his room much of the time. *Dwayne is designing a new boat*, was the fiction they all maintained.

Jean now sitting opposite her there, wearing a pair of neat blue slacks and a loose sea-green top, had become an older woman, a woman with dried skin and brown-spotted hands and an odour of stale perfume. *Always dab a little bit on here and there.* That Jean was her mirror image with different features, Almeida well knew. Your trouble, Almy, her mother had said, is you can see too much. And that, too, was true.

"Jean!" Well she had come out with the first part, the name. Her friend looked back at her slyly waiting for her to drop the other shoe.

"Jean. I want your advice. What would you do now, if you were married to Joe?"

"Do you mean you're going to hit him or something?"

"I've made some enquiries. Legal enquiries."

They could hear Joe's electric lathe through the wall. He was beginning something new. There he was next door, there he was, there he was sure to be, at eleven in the morning, chipping, splintering, working his way towards perfection.

When I've made one perfect one, I'll quit. Three years ago he had promised that. And that was when the faces were still in the basement and the wood chips had to be carried out in sackfuls on Fridays only.

"I know you tried to persuade him to move to the country."

"The housing market's down now."

"They're going to want to know why you didn't leave?"

"I've been everywhere I can."

Now that Jean was more of a critical spectator, understanding could be expected on some days and not others. This was a day when her affection was shown in the tea and the brittle home-made cookie. And how could you tell a friend that she didn't put enough shortening in her recipe, that oats swelled as they cooked, they sucked in moisture?

"Here. I'm offering you a room."

Tears came to Almeida. Tears she hadn't been able to shed in Vancouver or Jasper or Rocky Mountain House now made it hard for her to see. This was sacrifice. In Jean's neat and flowery home there was room for her, there was a space at least five foot nine and forty inches at the widest point wide.

Almeida said, through her tears, "I'd like another of these delicious cookies, please." She had come to her friend for advice and had been given love. It was very hard to bear.

"Well I mean it."

She touched Jean's hand and returned to the house next door. Her suitcase, she always managed with only one, was still in the hall. And the sound of the lathe was a high-pitched deterrent to conversation. Nevertheless she had to speak.

In their house, the faces looked at her from every wall and from the floor. Some of them were tilted, others frowned, some were in profile, others full face. And they were her own eyes that looked at her, but wooden, without irises, plain dead eyes like the eyes of ancient statues.

Joe sang as he worked. He was a happy ridiculous man. And that was why until now, until this moment when the chairs in the dining room were filled with replicas of her, when on every step there was a left head and right head, and the spare room was so full of heads the door would scarcely open, she had not driven him away. She had been the one to go, to pack up and say, *I'm going on a little trip, I'll be back soon.* And she had left him there singing and chiselling and answering the phone.

"Some man called," he said, looking up now from the bench in the kitchen. "Some man called Eric phoned. Eric. I asked him to spell it."

"When did he call?"

"Last Thursday, I think?"

"Did he say what about?"

"About a fishing trip."

"The travel agent?"

"He said his name was Eric."

"You could've told me before."

Joe was wearing old grey slacks and a shirt that had once been blue and a rag round his neck. He wore gloves now to protect his hands and worked more slowly than he used to. As she came past him, he turned the block of wood he was working on away from her as if it were a private letter, something not to be seen.

"Any offers?"

"I think I got it right, Almy."

"Can I look?"

"Not yet. It's not quite finished."

He took off his apron and set it down on the floor with a jangle of metal. The pockets for his hammer and his chisel and screwdriver had been stitched by her years ago after she had read about the wonder of hobbies, their help in curing depression, overcoming the ennui of a nine-to-five life, and their absolute necessity in retirement.

How pleased she had been to find him working there at his new bench in those first weeks when he was at home all day and she still had six months to put in at the store. And how pleased she had been to see how quickly his moods had lightened. He had taken to singing again and once she had caught him leaping about the room in a dance of celebration.

Now he sat down on the edge of a chair that contained two heads and listened. He listened to her traveller's tales without hearing, his eyes fixed on her face. At last when she had come down from the mountains and back through the valley, he said, "It's nice to have you home."

"I've been back two days," she said. She had cleared a month's laundry away, swept two months' crumbs up off the kitchen floor, and appreciated the fact that there were no heads in the bathroom.

"Staying now?" he asked.

His own face was younger and brighter than it had been. He had shaved that day and his hair was combed. There was a look of triumph to him. There was wine in the fridge that had not been there when she left. She leaned across to him and smiled and said, "Perhaps."

By the river, by the mountains, she had sworn to give it another try. There had been love in this house once. Love had shrieked its existence from the walls and the ceiling. The girls had not been able to stand it and both had left as soon as they could to build lives with loves of their own. But there had been love here, in these very rooms. And she had returned to remind him of that.

Either the heads go or I do. That had been an old argument of long ago. After she retired, she had said that. And he had come towards her with his chisel and explained that this work gave his life true meaning.

Later she would negotiate for space of her own. She would insist on boundaries while at the same time letting him know that his carving was improving head by head. Way back there in the early years, they had laughed together. They might do that again. They might travel and climb the easier mountains side by side.

Before she went to bed, she got a turkey out of the freezer. A small one for a festive meal to which she could invite Jean and Dwayne, and she would make, among other things, her special salad.

He came to bed a little while after her and took her in his arms and said nothing for a long time. Then he made love to her in a ritual fashion as though one of the wooden heads had sprouted a wooden body. But that too could change.

Leaving him in their bed, snoring, his face to the wall, she crept downstairs to look at the new head. She had to put the light on and then stand and listen to make sure she was alone before she could reach out and turn it towards her. It was of darker wood than the others and it felt sticky to touch, almost like skin. It was the head of a beautiful woman. He had given this one a lean nose, narrow cheeks, eyes with pupils, eyes that looked at her now, questioning her rights.

"Who are you?" she asked the head. After all it had ears. It had small ears, perfectly placed. Its mouth was uneven, the side of the lower lip had a slight cast to it as though it was drawn back, drawn in over the teeth. And there was an insolence, a kind of possession to this head, a feeling of power. Almeida set it down quickly. She knew exactly who it was.

She cleared a space on the floor so that she could lie down and calm herself. She breathed deeply and cast her mind around for pleasant memories. Times were when Joe had taken her and the girls to the park, when she had packed a picnic for them all and he had sung bright songs and played an imaginary guitar and all of them had joined in the chorus.

Her conscience was clear.

She had tried many times to stare him into reality.

She had only once stood over him with the chisel in her hand, tempted in that moment to change that face of his while he slept.

She went upstairs and put a nightgown and a tooth-brush into her flight bag and a photograph of the two of them in the old days standing in front of a palm tree in California. And she went down those steps and picked up her travelling case and opened the door and walked out of that house, quietly, before it got light. She walked to the road and began to run through the first fallen leaves, her wheeled case clattering along the damp sidewalk.

The sound of the wheels shattered the silence just as that woman had shattered their marriage. The wooden head, that last one, was the image of the only woman Joe had ever loved. His unattainable love. The woman who had ruined everything. The woman he had been trying to hold close to him for all these years. She was the rival, not all the carving, not all the faces, not the new pieces of wood he brought so carefully into the house. He had got it right at last. He had clearly carved out the face of the woman she should hate but could not. Herself! Herself in those first years. Herself at twenty-five. Herself when young. His one true love.

Walking Away

Almeida wasn't afraid of her daughters. Any time she felt set back by Geraldine's frown or disturbed by Harriet's uncompromising glare, she dressed the girls in childhood's grubby snowsuits and sketched in damp noses. Now she was confronted by both at once, the frown and the glare. She wasn't afraid of them but she knew when to be wary. Right now she had a sense of being set upon by two people who'd talked the matter over. And over.

Harriet spoke first, "We feel you should have talked to us before you acted."

"You encouraged him to get a hobby," Geraldine said.

"You of all people," Almeida began and stopped. In another life she would, she hoped, get credit for the many things over the years that she'd refrained from saying out loud. She didn't say to her older daughter that whenever she chose to leave Melvin, she would find a bed and a sympathetic ear with her mother. But Geraldine surely sensed this and had to be the more understanding.

Harriet, who strode about the world confronting fear
and misery, was harder to deal with. Problems in a marriage were trivial to her, the single one. You married the guy and, better or worse, you stayed with him. What was a quarrel, a little not-getting-on, compared with spending decades in a refugee camp or living in fear that the next shot might kill you? There was truth in this but it was a distant truth and they were dealing with the here and now. Silently, Almeida wished her younger daughter love.

"I don't feel I have to explain," she said. "But I can tell you that there are times when you walk away or go mad."

"What about Dad?"

Those were the words that made her want to scream out in this plush room so that the manager would come over and ask them to leave. *Where's all this freedom your generation goes on about? Where is choice? Where is, it's my life and I'll do what I like with it!* What was wrong with walking away leaving him lying there inhaling sawdust? He'd made enough replicas of her to keep him company for the rest of his life. And the heads never talked back. Chalking up another point to herself, she refrained from saying, *He'll be better off without me.* She did say, "He won't notice I'm not there."

"We think you're making a mistake."

Harriet pried open her sandwich as if, even here, there might be foreign objects, live things mixed in with the tuna. How she survived in Africa, in India, was beyond comprehension. She'd driven from Ottawa for this meeting and no doubt headed along the Trans-Canada highway planning how to gain her objective: To put her parents back together like comic salt and pepper shakers on a neat ceramic tray.

Four eyes, two blue, two greenish grey, were looking at Almeida. Harriet's lips were set in a thin line. Geraldine was giving her impression of a fledgling bird, mouth open, waiting.

Harriet, having found no animal life, no Band-Aid from the cook's finger in her sandwich, took a bite of it, chewed slowly and swallowed and then said, "Mom," in a definite and silencing way.

Almeida concentrated her mind on the outfit Harriet had chosen to wear for this encounter. At least it wasn't a set of army fatigues. The green jacket set off her colour and she wore it with a pair of navy slacks. What gene had given her that dark auburn hair and those eyes? No one in Joe's family, or her own. Almeida's mother had looked at her second grandchild as if she might be a changeling. And now she was behaving like one.

Geraldine set down her soup spoon.

To ward off the impending harangue, Almeida asked, "Was that good dear?"

No answer.

Harriet drew in a good deal of air and exhaled. She began again.

"Mom, we know you have reasons. But you and Dad have been together now for forty years. You're not—well, young any more. Surely you could accommodate—I mean you could sleep in my old room. How can you afford two homes?"

[21]

Ah. They feared having to cope with the decline of two separate old dummies instead of a pair. *You have her this week. I'll have him.*

"You don't seem to realise that without Dad you'll be lonely. It's well documented that lonely people are more susceptible to illness."

Consecutive funerals just far enough apart so that people couldn't stay over, the baked meats couldn't be saved or the coffin used twice. The economic approach.

"The logistics of this are that twice as much money will be spent on rent, heat, light, food."

Were they worried about the inheritance? Surely they knew there would be very little.

"Married people live longer. It's the comfort. The safety. On your own, you might be a target."

A target? For robbers and rapists and con men, all of them thrilled to know that she was on her own. A shout had gone round the underworld, *Almeida Kerwell is on her own and living at 331 Barton, apartment 403.*

"And there isn't anyone else?"

Aha! The cruel stepfather stepped into the picture. Though at their age he could hardly be a threatening figure. They feared no doubt a toyboy, someone their own age hanging round her, kissing her in public, creating gossip.

"Old people's minds decline quicker when they're on their own. Studies have proved this."

Alzheimer's disease. The dread of watching a parent go slowly but surely gaga. *What day is it mother? Do you remember yesterday?*

"Older people on their own don't eat proper meals."

So we'll sink into vitamin deprivation and lose the

use of our faculties and need to be pushed around in wheelchairs, moved to a home.

"Are you hearing all this, Mom?"

"More than you know."

Harriet looked at Geraldine who nodded her agreement with all that had been said.

Gerry, two years older had, curiously, early on, allowed Harriet to become the leader in their games. Was there something she and Joe should have done back in those years to give this child a better sense of her own role? At any rate it accounted, sadly, for Melvin.

"You're not saying much, Mom."

"This song has been going through my head. 'You have danced with that man, Ever since the music began.'"

"What has that to do with anything?"

Just like Joe's versions of her, their perceptions of him were stuck in one place. For years he'd been their strong father, hard-working, quiet. Now those outlines had dissolved into the fuzzy shape of an old man who moved more slowly. And the Joe they had never known, the persistent lover, the man who thought he danced like Fred Astaire, was beyond their imagining.

"I've come all the way from Ottawa."

"I know, dear."

She'd chosen the lounge of the King Eddy as a meeting place so that at least she'd be in a comfy chair through the ordeal. Behind Harriet's head hung a picture of a train in a snowy landscape. The gleaming perfect train was chugging to nowhere through fields of virgin white. A typical product of the School of Hotel Lobby Art.

"How's Sharon doing?"

"She's worried about her exams."

Another awkward silence fed on itself. They were waiting for her to say she'd been stupid and would at once return home. She felt like Joan of Arc, and like Joan she wasn't prepared to give in to her inquisitors.

"Well Mother, I have to say I think you're being selfish."

"What do you know about me? Who am I to you? I have a life. I am a person. Not just a mother. Wife."

"Sit down, Mom."

"You think you invented Women, the new woman. We've been out there for decades, in our way. And now, when I try to step out, you, the two of you, want to put me back in a box with a man who wouldn't notice if I turned green overnight."

She began to walk away from them.

"You've always walked away."

"I have not always walked away."

Their faces, looking up, were accusing. She returned to the table and sat down. The waiter, approaching, coffee pot in hand, backed away.

"Where are you going next?" she asked Harriet moving the conversation onto a different track.

"I'm not sure," Harriet said. "But how can I keep leaving with this on my mind."

Geraldine looked at her watch. "Tyler has soccer practice. I'll have to go soon. The kids've been worried about you and Granddad."

The pianist came in and sat down to play the billed 'live music'. He let loose a jumble of tunes that would have been moribund if it had been an animal. The perfect background to their thoughts.

[24]

Your father can look after himself very well. How many years have you got left? Doesn't that make it more urgent. Don't you see what you're doing, girls? He's managed when I've been away. Well if you're determined. Don't close the door on this, mother. Your father can look after himself very well.

They were nibbling at her mind, taking small mean bites, making her wonder if, indeed, she was being silly. If perhaps she should go back, sweep the sawdust out of the house and say to Joe, life will be like this from now on. Could she tuck her tail between her legs, move out of the neat apartment which was now her own home, when for the first time in her life she had a room furnished exactly in her way, and return to him? How could she tell Helen and Annie who had cheered her on and helped her find the new place that she and Joe were staying together for the sake of the children?

"Your Dad didn't have much to say when I told him I was leaving."

"He was asleep, Mom!" Harriet shouted drawing stares from tables nearby, stares which became sympathetic looks, women around them assuming that the daughter had come crying to her mother about a thoughtless lover.

"I have talked to him since."

"So is there someone else?"

Almeida thought for a moment before she said, "Yes."

Outraged grownups in dirty snowsuits stared at her.

"Yes. There is. Me."

Two sighs of relief.

Last year she'd gone to visit Harriet. *I'm going to Ottawa to see my daughter.* It had a nice sound. She'd set out thinking to please Harriet by this motherly gesture.

[25]

And knew, in five minutes of stepping into the apartment, without words being said, that Harriet had put off other plans. A dinner with friends? Dinner with a friend? She had, as the descending parent, disturbed a chance of intimacy, even maybe of romance.

'Where would you like to go?' Harriet had asked then. And now she was asking, in a harsher tone, "So what exactly do you plan to do?"

I plan not to get sick, not to become destitute, to seek out a useful occupation. Not to get run down in the street, if you must know. To live alone. To be lonely if I like. She didn't tell the girls about the job offer, even to put their minds at rest, because to mention it would jinx her chances. The woman called Andra, sitting secure in her office marked, Personnel, had looked at her kindly in a way that meant, *You'll do. You'll be all right*, and promised to let her know on Friday. She would be fine.

Then fear struck her. Would they, these two, draw away from her, now that she'd chosen to be single? If they'd said to her, at the beginning, before they'd ordered their food, *We will never speak to you again if you go on with this*, she would have caved in. That was the unbearable future. To lose these two women would turn her life to nothing, to ash, to garbage.

Suddenly, Harriet's stare dissolved and she said, "Where will we have Christmas?"

And Almeida laughed. She laughed so hard that people round about stared. She couldn't help it, and if the girls stomped out and left her there and then, it would be too bad. She looked away from them and tried to compose herself. She felt a hand on hers and knew from the touch that it was Gerry's. And Gerry was giggling. Tears hung in the corners of Harriet's eyes.

"Santa will come just the same, girls. Wherever I am. We'll go and have dinner with your Dad." And that was the nub of it. They were her children still and at thirty-four and thirty-six, they only wanted to know where they would hang their stockings on December 24th.

"Meanwhile I could go round and do a bit of cleaning one day a week for Dad."

"You have enough to do at home, Gerry."

Harriet said, "There's a homebody website on the net. It takes you through the day. When to make the beds. When to get lunch. When to clean the toilets."

"There's a time to clean toilets? Everybody in Ontario's cleaning their toilets at 10.15?"

"I was thinking of Dad."

"I keep telling you."

"But you'll think about going back, Mom?"

For sure she would think about it just as, now and then, she thought about the Arctic Circle, the Chaos Theory, and the lifestyle of pandas.

"Drive carefully," she said to her venturous daughter.

And to the other, "Take care, dear."

Harriet would drive home stewing over the fact that she'd got no definite answer. But confident that her mother would think things over and soon settle back into her right place. Geraldine would simply hope, hope that everything would turn out all right. Just as she hoped that the toad Melvin would one day turn into a prince.

Almeida sighed and drew her wool jacket closer round her. Her children walked away together. She admired their straight backs. Neither of them turned to wave. *Is mother watching?* They were quickly lost in a maze of high glass and concrete and she was on her own. She walked a little farther along King Street. She was free. She skipped right there on the sidewalk. A courier grinned at her as he chained his bike to a tree. She skipped once more, delighted to know that she still could.

Sometimes I Look at Younger Men

"Sometimes I look at younger men," Almeida said.

And she did. She looked at their biceps and triceps and quads in the gym, and at their still unfrightened faces. She saw that some of them had very hairy legs and others were smooth. She looked at young men on the street in their well-fitting suits or tight jeans. And at their hands and eyes. She looked at dark-haired ones and fair ones and those going prematurely bald.

"Sometimes," she said to Jean, "they look back at me."

But only Ivar when he looked back had told Almeida, in his awkward way, what he saw: a young woman in an older body trying hard to get out. His comment reminded her of Joe and his attempts to immortalise her young self in wood. But she smiled and held in her stomach, handed Ivar the files he wanted.

Like her, he slotted his twice-weekly trips to the Fitness Centre in the lunch break. Sometimes they walked there together from the office and then he mentioned how much he wanted to get on in the new country and how he missed his friends in Norway.

Almeida had kept Ivar's first note to her and pushed it across the table to Jean. Jean spread out the crumpled paper and saw that Ivar had written with true Scandinavian terseness: Mrs. Kerwell, there is not clips for the papers.

He'd been told, Almeida explained, that, in North America at least, God was still in the details.

Almeida had never been one of those people who could ration herself to one telling phrase and let *Come up and see me sometime,* or *My dear, I don't give a damn,* express a volume of feeling and thought. She spoke. She let words flow and her listeners could pick out what they chose.

Over lunch, she had begun a perfectly good conversation about the weather and worked through international conflict, pay-equity for women, the value of rehydrating cream, and had brought it round to her father's love of hunting and his cavalier driving habits.

"My mother could have written the original road-kill cookbook," she said to Jean who was sitting opposite eating spinach salad and listening to her in the way that old friends do. Tolerating the repetition, waiting patiently to hear something new.

"My father could drive quite well when he wanted," Almeida said.

He'd driven her down the highway to her wedding thirty-eight years ago without hitting a thing. But she had the impression that the wildlife on that day, hearing the sound of his engine, had backed into the forest out of the way.

"You know, like a movie rewound."

Jean nodded. And Almeida continued. Joe himself was a young man then, a boy of thirty with a fine round behind, firm pectorals and thick brown hair that caught the light. Almeida stopped talking for a moment and considered this picture. Then she moved on.

The romance with Ivar, if she dared to call it that since no mention had been made of love or sex by either of them, had begun on a Thursday or maybe it was a Wednesday. At any rate, the sun was shining through the windows of Combined Charities Inc., beams full of dust particles hit the papers and files. Both of them had reached for the same application. Their hands had touched.

When Jean suggested that she was responding to a deep and fleeting need, Almeida said, Garbage! Her life at the moment was full and pleasing. I mean you could have said that two years ago. Just after she'd walked out of her marriage. Those were bleak months and dry days. When she'd left Joe and his chisels and wooden heads, life hadn't exactly opened up like a fast river leading to the Sea of Opportunity. Some people said without putting it into those exact words, Well at fifty-six what do you expect! As if a flair for résumé writing and owning two decent outfits was not enough.

"As you know," Almeida told her friend. "I walked into that job at CCI as if I was the only applicant."

And there in the next office was Ivar, struggling with the language, reading every journal he could get his hands on, running around looking for help and advice, listening and then repeating phrases like a mynah bird.

The following week, she showed Jean his second, more intimate note. "Almeida," it read, "there are still not enough clips for the papers."

"What's with all the paper clips?" Jean asked.

"We have to gather material on would-be recipients and references and all kinds of letters and background."

"Computers?"

"Back-up. Hard copy. Loss of power. All kinds of reasons. The original documents have to be saved."

"And you and Ivar work at the same desk?"

"He likes to talk to me."

Almeida turned away from the sceptical look on her friend's face.

"I have to get back," she said.

No one round the office mentioned the fact that Ivar was young enough to want children. No one mentioned that he was married because no one knew whether he was or not. They took it for granted that somewhere near Oslo a tall blonde on skis was standing in the snow calling out his name in vain.

What Almeida didn't say to Jean, given Jean's attitude which could well be based on jealousy, was that Ivar had looked back at her at the very moment when she had begun to wonder if her gestures were ridiculous and if her phrases were out-dated. She had even begun to wonder if she looked like a man wearing women's clothes. Her face had taken on sharper lines the past few years; hairs sprouted one by one on her chin. Not that, she would have said to Jean if she'd been talking aloud, she had anything against transvestites. She just didn't want to appear to be one at that particular time.

[32]

Only that morning, Ivar had come into her office wearing running shorts and a sleeveless shirt and found her sitting at her desk staring into a mirror and not liking what she saw. He had taken her hand and kissed it in a way she associated more with French people than those from the chilly north.

She knew it meant nothing, but when he suggested that they have lunch together, it took all her self-control not to leap over her desk and hug him.

It wasn't what you'd call a date, sitting next to Ivar in the cafeteria. She talked to him and when she paused for breath, he talked to her. He was laughing because he'd read in *Time* that the Chinese had a learned committee for "The Investigation of Rare and Strange Creatures." Almeida wasn't sure if he considered her to be either or both or if he did, whether it was a compliment.

Later he made the remark about a sculptor and his block of marble and the figure trapped within it. But Almeida had heard that one before and couldn't help thinking that Ivar perhaps knew more about the language than he let on.

Almeida told Jean about her second lunch with Ivar, or was it the third, at least it was a Tuesday. It had to be Tuesday because it was the step class.

"We were eating tofu salad," she said, "in the café at the fitness place because they serve healthy food and we never have more than twenty minutes to spare. And Ivar told me that the Romans invented bingo."

"Fascinating," Jean said. And did not say, although Almeida could see she was thinking it, *You'd have been better off to stay with Joe.*

Almeida could still hear the sinister sound of wheels, little tinny wheels, following her along the sidewalk early in the morning, the day she walked away from her marriage dragging her suitcase.

Her children, forgetting the songs she had sung to them, the soup she had fed to them, the tears she had wept for them, remained distant. They had taken their father's side. Had she not told him to get a hobby? He had only done what she said! For that she had left him! And now, there she was cavorting, Geraldine said in reproach, with someone a third her age.

"Imagine," Almeida said to Jean. "Cavorting! Me. And he's not a third my age. That would make him nineteen."

"And a half," Jean said,

"And what does age matter? I can't help saying it, Jean. I know it's being said all the time. But age is only a number."

At work, Almeida listened to Ivar talk about Ibsen and the cold strong land he had left. She read *The Doll's House* and could see no happy future for that family. Those children would be scarred for life, she said to Jean, but not to Ivar.

When Jean phoned, Almeida's fingers made sticky marks on the receiver. Her herring salad was still not turning out like the picture in *Norwegian Cookery for Beginners*. The kitchen was beginning to smell like a fish factory.

The next week, Jean had some talking to do herself. It was Almeida's turn to listen. Jean told Almeida that something about Ivar had reached Joe's ears through all the noise he made with his hammer and lathe. He had taken a meat cleaver and cut her head in half. Jean and Dwayne had listened in horror to these deliberate thuds on the other side of the wall. Chop. Chop. Chop. Joe had gone round the house and cut in half all the wooden images he had made of Almeida since he took up carving. He had made her into a left and a right side.

Almeida, her spoon dipping into her broccoli soup, felt like a split personality. She drew a line down the centre of her face with her finger and wondered how different the two sides of her head were. When he cut her sculpted head in two had he realised at last that she was no longer that young version of herself that he had loved? Could he come to love her as she was now, older, with some lines on her face, with scads of experience and two thirds of life behind her? Was he finally aware that she was no longer the twenty-two-year old he couldn't bear to lose?

Jean was staring at her across the table but Almeida wasn't about to cave in.

"Good for him," she said.

"You're a hard woman," Jean replied.

Almeida put on a short blue dress with a tight skirt to meet Ivar for dinner. The rehydrating cream had softened her skin as advertised and the touch of lipstick gave her the look of an older aunt, not a long-married person with children but someone who has remained single and is gladly waving to the world from a good perch on the carousel of life.

At dinner, Ivar told her that more women than ever were marrying younger men. In Italy alone, he said, twenty percent of women married men eight to forty years younger than themselves. He had been given a copy of *Reader's Digest.*

Almeida invited Ivar to her apartment to look at her photographs of the fiords and glaciers in British Columbia that might remind him of his home. She waited, when she stopped talking, for him to lean across the table and ask her if she thought a romance with Andra in Personnel would be all right for him. But Ivar said no such thing. She waited for him to ask whether or not he should be more aggressive at the office. But he didn't say that either. She waited for him to hold her hand and tell her he was looking for a mother.

But Ivar told her that a thousand different kinds of birds inhabited the Galapagos Islands.

Attaching loops to the back, Joe was selling her profile for people to hang on their walls. So his hobby had after all become a profitable post-retirement occupation. Almeida called up her daughters to say to them in a pleasant way, I-told-you-so. But they were still uptight about her leaving their father and now betraying him with a young blond Viking. She heard envy in Gerry's voice and offered to baby-sit.

A dream more cheerful than a Bergman movie that had to do with warm dressing gowns and small cups of first-rate coffee began to invade her nights.

On the third Friday in March, a cold day, one of those winter-will-never-end Toronto days, Almeida met Jean at the Blue Bear Bistro.

She said hello and ordered a bagel with cream cheese and smoked salmon and the purée of vegetable soup to start.

After several minutes, Jean said, "You're not saying anything, Almeida."

Almeida answered, "There's nothing to say."

Ivar had gone. No word of farewell. No phone call. Nothing except the empty space his 180 pounds of tall blond youth had occupied at the office.

Jean didn't respond but reproach stood between them like an indigestible plate of nachos with cheese and sour cream.

"I have been foolish," Almeida said when they met the next week, sliding gingerly into the booth. In response to Jean's look, she said, "The rowing machine! I don't usually use it but it was there. And I thought, why not."

Ivar had been using her to learn the language, to try out his unusual phrases and had gone to a better life in Ottawa. Listening to her flow of talk was like an ESL course on disk, Andra had told her. Almeida stopped looking for letters or waiting for the phone to ring. Stopped wondering how she might justify marriage to a twenty-nine-year-old to her daughters.

She didn't mention Ivar's postcard to Jean the following week but the message looped through her mind like the words of an old commercial: "Almeida, thank you for learning me so much of English. Your many words has helped desirably. Kind greetings, Ivar."

Jean knew better than to ask questions. She talked instead about Dwayne's new job and how finally, he might be moving out to a place of his own.

Then she asked gently, "Will you go back to Joe?"

"Can he glue my head back together?"

"What's that supposed to mean?"

"It's not really me. I realised that. He was dreaming about all those glamorous women in movies in the forties and fifties. Merle Oberon, Rosalind Russell, Dietrich. The hair was a dead give-away. It wasn't me. It was who he wished I was."

"Everybody dreams, Almeida."

"Do you know what I dreamt last night? I don't always dream, but last night I dreamt I was climbing up the side of an iceberg. It wasn't easy."

Almeida felt tears coming but held on and stopped them in their tracks. She understood now that she was guilty of exactly what she had blamed Joe for; not being able to let go of that youthful image and accept the older man.

"All the same," she said to her friend, "I will go on looking at younger men."

And she would, not because she expected to sweep one of them off his feet and into her bed, but simply because it gave her a great deal of pleasure.

A Tribute of Memory

It was a Friday when Almeida saw her uncle on the
Dundas streetcar. She was sitting on one of the long rows
of seats at the back, and he was two rows ahead facing
forward. She had a good view of his profile and caught the
remembered look of elfin kindness. He was muttering to
himself, smiling a little. A blood-stained hanky was hanging from his pants pocket. She yearned to touch him. She
could hear faint whimpering sounds and realised they were
coming from her. She rode on three extra stops and watched
the old man get off at Sorauren. Her legs were shaking. She
didn't dare to get up in case she fell down and was carried
on to the terminus. At Dundas West she had to hand over
another ticket to ride back to her stop.

When she'd turned the key in her apartment door
and closed it and locked it, she made herself a cup of
coffee. Pictures of times she hadn't thought of for years

rushed through her mind, fast forward, rewind, fast forward, pause and hold. She cried and laughed aloud and cried again. She had her hand on the phone twice to call Joe. But Joe might hurry straight to her apartment saying to himself, *She needs me, she needs me*, and there'd be no getting rid of him.

She took out her bank book and looked at the balance. Joe had kept the old Dodge and till now she'd managed to get around easily enough on foot or on public transport. Joe was slow about putting the house on the market. He still hoped she'd come back to him. She'd have to get after him about it. With her share of the proceeds she'd be able to buy a small condo way out of town or maybe a large car which, if she became entirely destitute, she could live in.

"Mind you," she told Jean at lunch next day, "Uncle wouldn't have been seen wearing that kind of tweed hat and never a sweater. He was a jacket man. He needed his pockets. He liked to look smart."

"It wasn't exactly him," Jean said.

"He was talking to himself. He smiled once or twice as if he was remembering the time Aunt Zena went skating—she was seventy-five at least—and fell on the ice with her legs in the air screaming because her underwear was showing."

"Almeida!"

"And it turned out her ankle was broken."

The waitress set down soup and a sandwich in front of Almeida and broccoli quiche with salad for Jean. She looked at each of their faces as if expecting more from two regulars than their murmured thank-yous, but Almeida wasn't to be stopped.

"His shoes were very clean. He cleaned his shoes every day. The mark of a gentleman he used to say. I wondered if he was warm enough. It was only five degrees out yesterday morning."

I'll buy a car, small, nippy, used, she said to herself. She pondered on the last three words and wondered if they might apply to her, to parts of her anyway.

"There was a funeral," Jean said. "Six years ago. I remember you going to it. It was the year Dwayne moved back in."

But Jean hadn't seen the old man on the streetcar sitting on the aisle seat, surrounded by fragments of shared memory going back to the war; clear images of meals at a long table in the cool summer kitchen in the house on Bailey Street. Almeida could almost smell the bunches of fresh thyme hanging up to dry, see the bunches of purple grapes hanging from the vines in the backyard.

Making a move towards sanity as she saw it, Jean told Almeida that Dwayne was cheerful again. He had met an old friend and they'd been out for a drink, there was a faint chance of a job. Almeida said she would keep her fingers crossed. Jean's son was not so far making a success of his life. But was Harriet? Was Geraldine? How did you ever measure the success of children?

For their Sunday movie they picked a rerun of *The Streets of Laredo* at the Revue though Almeida was vague about going at all. Uncle George had thrown her routine into confusion. That kind of Western life was over surely, and right now she wanted relevance.

"What are you doing?" Jean asked, when Almeida stopped by the desk after they'd paid the bill. As if she was going to complain that her soup was watery or the service poor.

"I'm asking them to call me a taxi. It's this, or staying home," she said. "This or becoming a recluse. I'm afraid to go on the streetcar again. My Dad was one of seven."

Jean shook her head.

"And George was the youngest."

Waiting on the sidewalk, Almeida went on, "He called his daughters Star and Sapphire after a car. He drove me to work in it a few times. I felt like royalty."

"What happened to Star and Sapphire?"

"You think I'm making this up?"

"No. Only you haven't mentioned them before."

"I have. Sue and Martha. Poor Star. Six feet tall and her name was Star Towers like some apartment building. Changed her name to Susan when she started teaching. Sapphire called herself Sapphire Blue till she quit exotic dancing. She was good at it. For a few years. Martha now. Sells real estate in Kamloops. I told you."

"You never told me she was a stripper."

"I don't see Uncle George on the streetcar every day."

Jean said no thanks, she didn't want a ride, she had shopping to do and would walk. And Almeida sat back in the taxi and yes, just like this, she had sat back in the Star Sapphire and stared at the back of Uncle George's head, hair still cut military style, very little of it showing under his cap. That image was driven from her head by the scent of cut grass; the lost summer day.

It's a dull day, sun creeping in at the edges. A yellowish green hedge and a thick atmosphere like a smoky room. Toronto. Her two-week visit with her sister to the city.

And Uncle George is coming towards her and Jess with an ice-cream cone in each hand. That day always stopped there in her mind and never moved to evening, to dinner. There was nothing beyond the cone. Not even the flavour remained. He puts the cone into her hand. She closes her fingers round it. And that's it. Blank!

The taxi dropped her outside Happy Acres. The old folks had the tables set up and the cards ready. She had good cards but kept on losing. Her partner glared at her, but Mary, who was ninety-three and barely able to speak, stroked her hand as if she knew that something was wrong. Almeida felt her eyes fill with tears and when she'd had her cup of tea and a chocolate cookie, she asked the receptionist to call her a taxi and didn't stay to chat.

"See you next week," she said. And on the drive home she calculated the annual cost of taxis versus running a car.

"They talk of more snow," the driver said when she paid him.

Snow like shredded paper. Christmas that year they'd driven down to Toronto hardly able to see three feet ahead at times. Cars in the ditch on either side. Mom and Dad and Jess and her. Next day, sliding down the hill in the ravine opposite the house on a piece of cardboard, shrieking, laughing. Running into the tree. Crying. Being carried into the house. The snowsuit undone. *Let me see.* And Aunt Marge there loudly pushing uncle away. *I'll look after her, George.*

Almeida didn't often drink but since her mind was acting like a self-winding movie, she had to have something.

[43]

She poured a neat amount of Scotch into a glass over ice. Even during the trip to the kitchen, the memories didn't slow down. Figures, pictures, colours, danced around her like wasps. Another restless evening lay ahead, so she took off her skirt and sweater and put on her ratty green robe. The other one, the blue silk, she kept in its box for those times when all was right with the world. It was set, at this rate, to become a family heirloom.

You're like your mother. Who'd said that? In a voice of longing?

Who sang, *When I grow too old to dream,* in a voice that missed all the high notes?

Who said, *We don't speak about George,* in angry tones?

When had he become a man known by his absences?

Hungry, she grated the two squares of cheese that had turned hard in the fridge and made herself a toasted sandwich. Not the best thing for an older woman ten pounds overweight and barely able to fasten her new skirt. But who set those figures anyway? Skinny dieticians, that's who! Bad-tempered because they didn't get enough to eat. She put the sandwich on a plate with a slice of tomato and three radishes and sat down on the sofa again among the ghosts.

Uncle George in a smart black suit. After the war, he'd kept on driving. Chauffeur to a politician and then to the man who owned Carlo's and loved old cars. *Come for a ride in my car, honey.* Geraldine and Harriet were in school then, giving her a chance to work afternoons for Doctor Singh. Helen, seeing her arrive at the office in such style, had teased her for weeks about her sugar daddy.

In that car she'd felt like a princess and smiled, wanted to wave her hand to imaginary crowds. Uncle George looked at her in a sheepish way when he opened the door for her. One day he made her a present of a pink silk scarf. He said very little on those rides. How did he know when she had to be at work. Had she told him? Had he come to the door of the house in Don Mills and said, *I'm sorry to hear about your mother. She was a lovely woman?* And cried a second time?

It came into her head, arrow-straight then: The cone is strawberry-flavour, her favourite. She's wearing a lemon-coloured dress. And Jess is in jeans because Jess is always in jeans, and Jess is running on ahead. He watches her lick the melting ice cream and Jess keeps on running.

In those days he had hair and was soldierly and tall. About to leave for Europe. Another absence.

There was a later Christmas, she and Jess were maybe sixteen and eighteen. Christmas, a smaller gathering than usual. Aunt Marge cooked the turkey. George was away, they said, but didn't explain. The adults murmured about the war affecting people different ways. Even for a long time after there might be no end to the terrible effects of fighting, of loneliness.

She and Jess had talked it over and decided that he had gone out of his mind and was in the loony bin.

The phone rang and startled her back into real time.

"Hello?" she said, half expecting Uncle George to answer.

"It's me, Joe."

"Oh."

"Are you all right? You sound funny."

"Fine. I'm watching a mystery, that's all."

"We have to go to the bank Monday, remember. They need your signature."

"Will you pick me up at work, please?"

"Sure, of course, Almy. I'll be there."

"Twelve. I'll be in the lobby."

They're round the long table again in the summer kitchen. In his gentle voice, Uncle George is talking as usual about something he refers to as The Great Cosmic Plan. He's the only person she and Jess know who talks about a future, a large view of the meaning of life. He is saying that we, meaning people, are losing what we have because of sloppiness. We let things go slipping and sliding until they're in a bad way and then get in a panic. Our remedies, he's saying, are worse than the disease.

Her father's voice, a loud echo in her mind: *I'll have some venison by the end of the week.* And her mother's response: *Don't give any to the Milsoms, they've no idea how to cook it.*

Uncle George looks as if something is lost while they discuss ways to cook venison or pursue the shortcomings of the Milsom family. And then he sits silently, glancing across at her mother from time to time as if there is a tale to tell.

There was a prolonged absence in which he married another wife, one with a fancy name. The rarely mentioned Angelica, mother of Sue and Martha.

An uncle known for his absences. *Where's Uncle George?*

[46]

Faces turned away. There were whispers in later years of harsh treatment from his new wife, his children. Nothing confirmed.

The sun came out from round the edges and brightened that old summer day. Jess is still running on ahead. Uncle George is sitting beside her on a wall. He is wearing a holiday shirt and beige slacks. He has his arm round her. *You're a lovely girl.* And Jess is a stick figure in the distance. *You're my lovely girl. Your mother was a lovely girl.*

Almeida looked in the drawer for her photographs. First in the book, her High-School Graduation Picture. She stared at it. That white dress had taken weeks to make, pulling out stitches, deciding on the navy trim, wanting it perfect. She looked pretty good. Her face already a woman's face, not much different from the one Joe had tried so hard to replicate in wood.

She'd turned from the platform to smile at her Dad's camera and looked out over the crowd aiming for a noble profile and there he'd been. Tears running down his cheeks. Uncle George! She'd almost stumbled and Mrs. Peak had leaned forward and held her arm and said in her ear, "Steady now, Almeida."

Afterwards she'd pushed her way through the crowd, searching about, trying to find him among all those people spilling out into the corridor. The air was full of words and names. *Congratulations Jean, Tom, Maggie. We did it.* Arms reaching out. *It's over. School's out. We've made it.*

It was around twelve years later, knowing somehow where she lived, that he called and offered to drive her to work. And never during those drives, did he say a single thing that might explain why. He said very little. As if he was wanting to tell something but couldn't find the words. And she sat in the back seat, knowing there was something he wanted to say but not able to help him out. He only seemed glad that she would be there with him.

The sun is full out; the ice cream has dripped over her hands. Strawberry ice cream leaves a sticky mark. Oh my, Aunt Marge says, and takes the dress away to wash.

Almeida called Jean and suggested lunch at a different place next week.

"Will you be arriving in a limo?" Jean asked.

"I'll be on the streetcar," Almeida replied, figuring that her friend maybe had a right to be sarcastic, not being in possession of all the facts.

And who was in possession of all the facts? The people who might have given her other pieces of the puzzle were dead. There was only her own unreliable memory.

She wasn't sure if when he took her face in his hands on that summer day, Uncle George was seeking a kiss or seeing a beloved face in hers. She had no sense of harm done but only a transferred feeling of loss so strong that she had cried out and run to the house.

She decided to hold on to the image of Uncle George among the parents on Graduation Day at Huntsbridge High. The look on his face, as she now recalled it, was a mixture of sadness and pride. Pride through tears. A pride that matched that of all the parents in the hall. The other pictures could be returned to the storage bin at the far back of her mind.

On Monday, she waited at the TTC stop after work again. It had begun to rain. The streetcar was making its snaky way into sight. Almeida knew that if she saw the old man again she would smile at him and maybe even wish him a good day. She hoped that wherever he lived now, people were treating him with kindness.

The Unknown Russian

Almeida saw Ivan Davidovich in the crowd again. This time he was wearing a cheap imitation astrakhan hat and a drooping grey raincoat. Around him stood tired women in scarves and men in desperate attitudes. They were demonstrating outside the Kremlin because they hadn't been paid for three months. Nearly eighty years since the Revolution and they were in the same poor state as before nineteen-seventeen. Guarantees had come and gone, and that morning a businessman had been shot down in Moscow, gangster-style. The people had been sold a wild kind of democracy—freedom to fear without prosperity. Almeida shook her head.

When her mother was a girl, skipping rope in Smiths Falls, the Russian workers were not being paid and their lives were wretched. Here they were again. This time on TV for all the world to see. Where would they be when Geraldine's kids were grey-haired and retired from their three-day workweeks? What would be happening to the Russian people then?

As a child she'd loved the painted Russian doll that came apart to reveal another, and inside that another and then another, smaller but always the same. And in the centre, was the smallest, the solid one, the one that couldn't be taken apart. Jess one day had taken the toy and painted every one of those smiling babushkas black. "How could you be so mean to your sister?" their mother had asked. Almeida was still waiting for an answer.

She switched off the TV and sat back helplessly in her armchair and sipped the coffee she'd made too quickly—too little coffee, too much milk— and wondered what Ivan Davidovich's real name was and whether he was married to one of the headscarved women. Whether he drank too much vodka. Whether his children were kind. She'd pointed him out last night to Jean when they were watching the news, and Jean had said that since he was in the crowd every time he was probably a government spy. But Almeida knew despair when she saw it and didn't bother to argue.

Joe had called first thing and asked her to come with him to look at a bachelor apartment. She knew it was a cunning move on his part and told him next week maybe. He said he had to get the car fixed. So for a time at least he'd be happy in some garage or other. Grease and metal, noisy tools. Admiring new models way out of his price range.

She went back to considering the Russians. Ukrainians, Kazakhs, Chechens, all separate now, all trying to be independent. Thinking about them with sympathy was no help at all. They couldn't feel her compassion. The few dollars she might send to the man in the crowd would get stolen *en route*. Even if she knew his real name and his address.

How were he and Mrs. P. paying their rent, buying food, getting warm boots for their children? Her thoughts were leading her along the crazy route that could bring on headaches and depression and trips to old movies with Jean.

She picked up the phone and pressed number five on the pad and when Geraldine answered, said, "I'll take you out to lunch."

"I'm all right, mother," Geraldine said.

"Twelve o'clock. Harry's Bagel."

"I don't like bagels. I'm not eating lunch."

"I'll see you."

"Really mother!"

When she put the phone down, Almeida hoped Geraldine didn't know she was number five in the memory after Harriet, Joe, Jean, and the doctor. If she felt close to death or at least very ill, she would change the order and put Joe first, then Geraldine followed by Harriet, then Jean, Jess, and the doctor last. Best to leave the family as little to grieve over as possible.

How can you be thinking about such trivial things, she said to herself. *You have too much time.*

The first week of vacation had been full of deferred projects, there were goals, objectives. But this second week was like a rehearsal for retirement. Life would open before her like the jaws of a great animal. She peered in and saw weeks and months without end. Infinite time! Time to consider lives she could in no way help. Time to wonder what Comrade Prishchev would be like in bed. The way ahead could easily lead to the terrors of completion; an apartment perfectly clean; a closet containing nothing except what was useful; drawers arranged. Hours would be spent, hands on lap, waiting for dust to settle so that she could begin to wipe the surfaces again. She left her coffee mug in the sink to ward off that awful image and put her coat on.

She got to Harry's early. She liked to sit in the corner and listen to the humming chant of young parents murmuring their worries, business people marking out their territory like dogs but with loud barks instead of piss. She took a look at the people sitting on their striped chairs and wondered how often they had sex and if they enjoyed it when they did. The man in the corner for instance, currently unemployed, was looking at the want ads and marking them with a pen. Did he pick up women and take them to motels now that his afternoons were free and did he tell them sadly that he was on the scrap heap of life?

Geraldine hurried in, smart in a new-looking dark green jacket and slacks, slyly glancing round as if she too was taking a secret survey.

"Good to see you, Mom. What's this all about?"

"I can have lunch with my daughter without it being about something, surely."

"I can't stay long," she said. "What are you having? I'll just have coffee."

"Bagel and cream cheese. And coffee. You eat something dear, you look a little . . ."

"I look fine. You're a bit pale yourself."

"I'm worried about the oppressed," Almeida said.

[53]

The waitress, smirking at something the man in the corner had said to her, came to take their order.

When she went away, Geraldine said, "What did you say, Mom?"

"I worry about people being miserable. Whose lives are in chaos."

Geraldine said, "How did you know?"

People's eyes don't *fill* with tears, Almeida thought looking at her daughter, they film over with water, they see you through a curtain of liquid. She reached for her daughter's hand.

"Melvin. The person—he always refers to her as a 'person' in the office. He stayed late. She calls him. Nothing happened, he says. What does he mean by that? What kind of nothing?"

Almeida patted her daughter's hand while she tried to sort out the right thing she might say without bringing on a cry of *You don't understand.* Or worse, *You have never understood.*

She wanted to say, *He's an oaf, drive him out of your house. Wait till it rains and then throw his clothes onto the street. Empty the bank account. Keep the car. Rip him apart.*

Geraldine sniffed. "I know what you think. But."

Oh and in that 'but', such a world of thought. Geraldine probably thinking that her mother had foolishly left her father and was living apart from him still for frivolous reasons. At their age they should live together in harmony and make their way with dignity to the end of life.

Geraldine, the perfectionist in the family, had to make her marriage work. She was not prepared for failure. She knew what was required. She obeyed the rules and expected life to be fair in return and it hardly ever was.

Almeida held back her sermon on marriage being these days an unreal thing, how perhaps it always had been. People grow older and change. How was it possible not to become, over a length of time, incompatible? How? Her own example, walking out on Joe, should have told her daughter something.

Taking a deep and fearful breath she said, "Gerry. What do you want to do? What seems right to you?"

"Nothing. Nothing seems right." She took two sips of coffee and pushed the cup away.

A pattern of the younger woman's days stood between them like a range of cutout dolls. Geraldine, getting up early, setting out breakfast for her family, entertaining hope. The kids rushing out to school. Melvin at the last minute picking up a coffee mug, reaching for a muffin, leaving Geraldine alone with the paper, the phone, the rag-end of the early morning. Tidying, considering dinner, and off to work herself. Fridays her day off. The weekend bringing a chance of good times, or maybe only the memory of good times.

Almeida tried to reach out to her daughter but it was like sending money to the unknown Russian. Her feelings of love and sympathy could easily get lost even in the short space across this little table.

I know how it is, she might have said. *I have been there. Like the U.S. President, I share your pain.* But it wasn't shared pain. Her present pain was a knife stuck in her heart because she could not, however she might try, give her daughter instant happiness. A smooth sailing. An easy passage through a life lit with the stars of success and constant love.

[55]

"And his mother," Geraldine said, "stopped in on Friday and came right into the kitchen to see what was for dinner. Lifted the lid off the pot."

"Dottie always did like to taste things." Almeida pictured Geraldine's mother-in-law bending over a cauldron with a ladle and sipping the broth to see if there was enough bats' blood in it. "Did she say it needed a tad more frog sweat?"

"Mom!"

Gerry had turned away and was looking out of the window when the man came over to their table.

"Hey Gerry," he said and went on standing there, awkwardly.

"Stephen."

Almeida said, "Hello."

The man bowed as if he'd stepped out of an old movie and said, "This must be your sister, Gerry. Aren't you going to introduce us."

Gerry said, "Stephen Wong, this is my mother, Almeida Kerwell."

"Nice to meet you Mrs. Kerwell. I'll be getting along. I was just passing. I'll be back later most likely."

He moved away and Almeida felt her daughter's thoughts follow him.

"A friend?"

"He's nobody," Gerry said. "His kid's in Tyler's class."

But her eyes watched the man move very slowly to the door. There was a pause. A vibration. Geraldine spoke with more energy in her voice.

"You sounded worried when you called, Mom."

"I was thinking about the Russians."

Geraldine looked round as if there might be Stalinists

in the room. Or perhaps, at best, some Cossack dancers there to entertain. She said, "Why them?"

"Their lives, the ordinary people's lives, never seem to get any better."

"I expect they have their good times." She looked round again and there was silence.

Almeida tuned in to the family at the nearest table. Their voices were softly musical as if their conversation could be made into a choral piece. *Oh God,* she thought, *I should be working.* She said to Geraldine, "I'm sorry if you had plans. I'm sorry about Melvin."

"I told you, Mom. It's something I'll work out, all right? Just keep worrying about the Russians."

In that way she shut her mother out leaving her with too few pieces to make a whole story. She kissed her, leaning down slightly as if Almeida had shrunk. And Almeida watched her daughter hurry round the corner towards the parking lot. She pushed away the rest of her bagel and went out into the street.

"Watch out!"

"Sorry!" She had nearly fallen over a stroller low to the ground, pushed by a young woman whose face was set in angry lines.

Marriage! Fitting people together in halves. Pairing them off. What kind of jigsaw puzzle mentality made human beings do that? She began to walk very slowly down Yonge Street. It was two years since she'd moved away, out of the double bed, out of the house, their home. Joe wanted her back. Wanted her to help him recover some of that old joy they'd once had. Yet at this very moment across town in the used car lot he was looking for something with less mileage on it. And in Moscow, the unknown Russian was looking for a better way of living. The promise had not been fulfilled. And was there a reason why those Russian dolls had to come apart before the next one could get out?

When she got to St. Clair, she turned and walked back to Harry's to get a couple of bagels for next day's breakfast. She pictured herself slicing them with care. An article in last Sunday's paper told of the number of weekend casualties there were in New York from people mindlessly cutting their bagels and the knife going straight into their hands, the soft skin between the thumb and first finger.

She was at the door of the café when she happened to look in the side window and there was Gerry, a salad on a plate in front of her. She was talking to the man called Stephen. Stephen. A nice name, a name of kings and saints. And his face as he smiled was pleasing, interested. *Oh*, she wanted to shout through the glass to Geraldine, *he'll be interested till he gets what he wants. Be careful, child of mine.*

Nothing changes, Almeida thought as she turned around to walk quickly away without buying the bagels. And then she contradicted herself. Of course things changed! They altered shape, got lost, shaken, re-arranged. But then, mostly, unless some effort was made, they settled down into a pattern very similar to what they'd been before.

Tomorrow morning, first thing, she would call the volunteer agencies, take a course, renew her membership at the gym so that at the end of the week there would be some goal achieved. A little touch of triumph. No more daytime television. Her days of retirement would have meaning, perhaps even a touch of pleasure in them.

[58]

Today she was simply glad to have seen her sad daughter laughing. And she hoped that maybe Ivan Davidovich Prishchev found time in a corner of his life to fling out his legs in a dance of lunatic joy.

Men Like That

"Men like that should be buried in backyards," Almeida said.

Jean hesitated for a moment before she replied, "I don't think I'd go that far."

"We are too old for this."

"What have we ever done?"

"Lots," Almeida answered though she knew, because she'd been thinking about it that very morning, that her life had not been as unselfish as she would have liked. Sacrifice and denial were not words that would be used at her burial service and it was a bit late now to start building a memorial. On the other hand, in church and Sunday school they had made it clear, if she was remembering it right, that it was never too late to begin. She didn't mention these thoughts to Jean.

Their usual restaurant was closed for renovation.

They'd walked down the street to The GreenWay and arrived with frozen lips. Inside they were overwhelmed by trails of leafy plants and servers with a larger than normal complement of teeth.

Almeida stirred her spinach soup hopefully and made patterns in the green slime with fat-free sour cream.

Jean said, "I hear them through the wall."

"There is a network of social services."

"Oh sure, they're all bogged down with cases."

"This government!"

"Don't start, Almeida."

Sprouts from the veggie sandwich were hanging out of Jean's mouth so that she looked like a walrus. Friends, Almeida thought, came in various shapes and degrees. Helen had worked beside her in Doctor Singh's office for twelve years but decades had gone by and they saw each other rarely. Besides, Helen had taken to playing bridge and her talk was all of last night's hand and the sins of her partner. Annie's Emma had gone to school with Gerry. When they met now, they talked about grandchildren, showed each other photographs, remembered the kids' school-days but that was the extent of it. Jean was the perfect accepting and loyal friend whose only flaw was that she put her x in the wrong place on the ballot paper. Jean in her wrongheadedness saw the same flaw in her.

"All I'm saying, Almeida, is they're not going to come out because a neighbour thinks there's something wrong."

"They might."

"They'll see it as spying, gossip."

"That's how most cases get reported."

"They don't come out for what might happen. Only for what has happened."

Spinach is good for you. The soup reminded Almeida of her mother and she wished she'd ordered a salad.

"We've gone on too long," Jean said, "being passive."

"What about the people on the other side?"

"They both play in the symphony. They're out evenings. Sleep half the day."

"She must have relatives."

"They seemed like such a nice couple when they moved in. He wouldn't let her carry the heavy stuff. I took them a cake and offered them coffee."

"So you could snoop," Almeida said.

She looked at her friend and saw determination. Jean had heard cries of distress and knew what they were. Years ago she'd run to Almeida for help. And now, as if life were a relay race of good deeds, she felt it was up to her to pass this benefit on to another troubled woman. Jean's late ex-husband, when confronted, had run back to his loving mother who saw only a perfect man with perfect manners; the good son.

At the time, on one dark summer day, Almeida had made Jean laugh by telling her that the pods of the laburnum were poisonous and both of them had known that, for a fraction of a moment, it wasn't a joke. Both of them had envisaged the soup, green like this soup, in which they might have disguised the bitter taste.

If Jean had feared seeing symptoms of violence in her own son, she'd never mentioned it. Dwayne's marriage had broken up through his inertia; a different kind of cruelty.

"If you want to continue with this, I'll need cake. Not here, it's probably made of parsnips. I want something made with butter and cream and chocolate."

"If you could hear them."

"And you're sure it's not the TV you're hearing through the wall?"

"I've seen her face."

"Well then."

They left the warm café and cold struck at them. Tongues of ice licked across the path, waiting to trip the old and unwary. They cursed the laggards who didn't clear their few yards of sidewalk. The Saturday shoppers walking towards the lake scrunched their faces against the wind. From under his blue blanket, the man looked up at them. He lay there most days against the stone of the building. His eyes held no expectation of rest or of kindness or of Spring. In the face of such defeat, many people walked on. Almeida stopped this time and rummaged in her purse for a two-dollar coin. And knew, even as she gave it him that it was a token, a useless offering. Across the street, under a piece of sacking lay another outcast. In this rich city these frozen statues, monuments to lost lives, provoked no comment; no one marched on their behalf. They had no vote.

When they got to the Blue Rose, Almeida turned away from the dessert menu.

Jean said, "Lunch once a week is our only extravagance, Almeida. We hardly ever spend more than twelve dollars."

"I'm not as hungry as I was, that's all."

Reaching across the table with her coffee spoon, she took a chunk of Jean's *Chocolate Indulgence*.

It melted into her, warmed her, sharpened her mind, and increased her doubts about Jean's project. Setting aside her slight vow to be more helpful, she expressed the practical view: Interfering in marital arguments often led to being turned on by both sides. But then Jean used the word, *abuse.*

"It's not as if he abused you," her own daughters had said when she left Joe. She'd wanted to say then that there was more to abuse than a punch in the eye but saw now that it was a frivolous response and was glad she'd held it back.

"Can we leave it overnight?"

"It's the weekend."

"I don't like to remind you of this, but we're two elderly women."

"That doesn't mean we have no conscience."

"I haven't been to the health club in weeks."

Back in her apartment, Almeida knew of sixteen reasons why they should forget the whole thing and go to the new James Bond movie instead. But Harriet stared at her from the frame on the bookshelf and her mouth seemed to form the word *coward.* From that word came others to remind Almeida of all the fearful things that happened in the world because no one moved to help. *You always walk away, mother.*

"We're two older women," she repeated aloud to the empty space but it sounded weak, a poor excuse.

She left a message with Sharon to tell her mother that Gran was spending the night at Mrs. Wiley's. Not that Geraldine phoned often these days but if she found her mother out at ten, or at eleven, she would call Joe and set alarm bells ringing all over town. They had decided that in her new single life she was not quite in her right mind and if out late at night would most likely be standing naked on the parapet of the Bloor Street Bridge. To the family, a woman crazy enough to leave a perfectly good man after forty years was capable of any mad act.

She put a nightgown and toothbrush and face cream and change of underwear into her overnight bag. Dwayne was up north checking out another job opportunity. She and Jean could have a pyjama party. She packed cheddar that was past its date but not yet green, and crackers. Jean would have bought gin on the way home.

She changed into slacks and an old sweater and slipped on her running shoes. If Jean was right, they might have to move fast.

On the subway train going west, she recalled that Jean had moved. She had to get off at St. George and go in the other direction. Jean's new townhouse might have all the advantages of modern living but it was nearly at the end of the line. If it had been decently sound-proofed, Almeida wouldn't be out on a fool's errand on this wintry night.

"Perhaps they're rehearsing a play?"

"This isn't like you, Almeida. I've always thought of you as my brave friend. Who would dare to do things."

"I've grown older. I have more sense. And when I look back, I haven't done that much, so I don't know where you're getting 'brave'."

Jean laid down a run in hearts and said, "My game."

She topped up their glasses and put the television on to watch the "Antiques Roadshow" but kept the sound low.

[65]

It was ten o'clock when the row began next door. A raging voice. A cry. A louder cry. A cry that couldn't be ignored and a thud—a body falling.

Almeida was first to the door and started to climb over the low wall; she held back for a moment when her leg stiffened and she had to wait for the pain to stop. There was no time to fear being pushed back and hit by an angry husband. Jean got ahead of her and knocked on the door. A wailing sound came from the other side of it. And then the door opened. Almeida moved forward and stood by her friend, ready.

Deanne's cheek was bruised and she was holding her arm against her body. Her eyes were staring, fit to fall out of their sockets. There was a red stain running down her grey sweater. She said nothing but let them follow her down the hall. A slight woman, she moved quickly.

"It's Dougie," she said. "I knew he didn't like it but why should he always have what he wants?"

Dougie was lying on the floor, his face peaceful, his feet nearly touching the counter at one side of the little kitchen. He lay there with blood and what looked like pieces of brain round his face, green, yellow, black. Almeida swallowed hard. Deanne stared down at the body.

"I hit him with this," she said, holding up a skillet. "What'll I do?"

Almeida recalled her casual remark to Jean earlier in the day. She shuddered. She could in a moment be hacking through the frozen ground, dragging the body outside, helping to heap the earth over a corpse. Or freezing him till the earth thawed in spring. They would clean the kitchen, burn the clothes, and every year have a secret meeting to gloat over their undiscovered crime. They would buy a rose bush to plant over Dougie. Maybe two as he was easily six feet long.

If they called the police, the weight of a trial, of jail would hang over this sad young woman. But there was right and there was wrong, it was said. Justice and injustice. Who made these rules? Jean was already at the phone, calling 911. She asked for an ambulance.

Dougie opened his eyes. He was trying to push himself up but kept falling back onto the floor.

"I didn't mean it, Deanne," he said. He saw the mess beside him and howled. Deanne had backed up against the wall.

"You slipped and banged your head," Jean said. "Deanne came to fetch us. There's an ambulance on its way."

"I hit you with the skillet," Deanne shouted. She threw it onto the floor nearly hitting him again.

He growled like an animal and then began to cry.

"What've you done?" he whimpered, looking at the mess on the floor.

"It's ratatouille. Remember? You said you weren't going to eat that muck."

"Well, would you?" he looked at Jean pleading.

"And your wife ran into a door!" Almeida said.

He put his arm over his face as if to hide from them all.

The paramedics wanted to take Deanne too, but she refused to go. They checked her face and told her to use heat on her shoulder for fifteen minutes and then use an ice pack.

In Jean's living room, she sipped gin and tonic and held the heating pad to her arm.

"Come back to my place," Almeida said. "I have a pull-out couch. He won't know where you are."

"There are shelters," Jean said, with a warning look at her friend.

"I'll be OK."

"I have a daughter your age. You can't go back. He'll resent what you did. He'll be mad."

Deanne had one of those narrow faces, a rare shape, which made her eyes seem large; her mouth when she smiled a wide vee. She'd taken off her stained sweater and put on a jacket. She said she hoped the bruise on her face would subside before Monday. They would say things at the office.

Jean suggested she call the police and talk to them anyway.

"I hit him," Deanne replied.

"Self-defence. He hit you first."

"Now he knows I can."

"I don't think," Almeida began but stopped. She'd been going to say that Dougie might then lash back harder. Wars began that way.

When the call came from the hospital to say that Dougie was stitched up and ready to come home, Deanne refused to go and fetch him. She put down the pad and thanked them both for coming round and Jean for the gin. She was a polite child in that moment. But there were no hugs, no response woman to woman. To her perhaps they were just two nosy old interfering neighbours.

They watched her go down the path.

Jean put the kettle on.

"Will she stay with him?" Almeida asked.

"She could've killed him."

"We wouldn't have been able to dig a grave till March, maybe April."

"It's all very well for you. You were fortunate," Jean said to her.

Almeida said nothing. Fortunate in that gentle Joe had never hit her? Compared to Dougie, Melvin was saintly, Joe was a dove, even her own father attacked only 'fair' game. Except that one time. And that one time was an accident.

She lay down in Dwayne's narrow bed, surrounded by his posters of other worlds and wondered if Deanne had told her mother. A glimpse of their wedding photograph on the sideboard next door had shown proud parents, a handsome couple, a sunny day. She dozed off and woke suddenly, her arms aching for no reason except that in her dream she'd been carrying a heavy weight up a steep hill.

The sound of a taxi roused her. She got up and went to the window. Dougie was walking towards his front door; he rattled it, shook it, cried out, "Deanne!" There was no answer. "Please. I love you, baby." He thumped the door again. "Come on. I'm freezing to death out here." The door opened slightly. He went inside. Almeida sat there watching. There was no sound. No fearful Deanne came running out of the house.

What if she and Jean hadn't interfered? What good had they done? Deanne was stunned but not hysterical. She would have pulled herself together and called the ambulance. She had gone back to wait for him. By now they had called a truce and were probably making love, careful to avoid each other's bruises.

[69]

She and Jean had made no difference. None at all. Their achievement, if there was one, lay only in the fact that Dougie and Deanne knew they were there, knew that next door an older woman was alert and watching. And perhaps that was all it took.

Mona Lisa Smiled a Little

Almeida was no psychologist but she knew a symptom of compulsion when she saw it. And she knew enough not to say to her new friend, *Have you had this problem long?*

"Felicity," she began.

The woman stopped her. "I've changed my name since I saw you last week. I changed it to Mona because I could truly see no chance for happiness ahead. The kids seem to prefer Steve's new girlfriend to me. She gives them candy and lets them watch TV all weekend."

Almeida thought, but didn't say, *This too will pass.* The problems of this generation were almost too much for them to bear. They'd achieved a freedom, a lifestyle, for which they'd been given no operating manual. In their search for happiness, they'd been led too far into the forest and birds had eaten the breadcrumbs off the path. On television every evening, thirty-year-olds who should have known better saw a face they liked, made sure the other was 'clean', and hopped into bed with him or her. Three days later, they broke off the relationship because the other ate salad for breakfast or squeezed the toothpaste tube from the middle. It was a jungle in which creatures sniffed each others backsides and jumped them if they liked the smell. You had to feel sorry for them.

The contrary-Mary in her mind decided just then to ask, *So what was your point in leaving Joe, Almeida?* She ignored the question and paid attention to the moment.

Here she was on a Saturday morning being asked for help by a woman who was smart, professional, young, and who had just changed her name to Mona. That she had a tendency to talk like a book probably hadn't helped the ex-Felicity. Maybe her Steve had simply gone to another section of the library and said, *I want something easy to read, something in large print, please.*

In bed, yesterday's Felicity had said things like, *Steven, our lives are not developing in a progressively meaningful way. What is your concept of our partnership as we head towards the millennium? We need to reexamine the baggage that each of us brings to this relationship and take correctional steps in order to.* By which time Steven had probably pulled his pants on over his pyjamas and run out the door.

"Mona?" Almeida said. "Well, she did smile a little."

But Mona had slipped from her seat and gone over to the wall. She was reaching across the heads of two people in a booth, her scarf dangling into their basket of bread, and setting straight a picture of totem poles in a forest of tall firs.

"Sorry," she said when she sat down again. "What were you saying?"

"Mona. Mona Lisa. She did smile."

"Not from happiness. You only have to look at the eyes."

They'd met at the Food Bank. Volunteering there was one of Almeida's steps to prove that she was a fairly useful citizen. Standing side by side, she and Mona had been casting out packets that were open and cans that were past their date, and Felicity had said, "Are these generous donors trying to solve the population problem?"

Almeida had laughed. Felicity had snapped, "It's disgusting."

Almeida had answered, "What's disgusting is that we have to do this. That all these people are in need."

They'd turned from their work then and looked at each other. Almeida had seen a young woman wearing a neat grey pantsuit, little make-up, and a tragic face. The fact that the then Felicity took twice as long as she did to pack one box, seeking the perfect shape to fill each space, might have told her something. But all she had thought at the time was that the young are precise.

And what had this Felicity/Mona, sitting opposite her now, pulling at one strand of her fair hair, seen in her but an older woman in a blue dress that made no nod to fashion, scented with old-fashioned lavender. If she'd happened to see a woman with experience and even wisdom, it would be cruel at this time of her distress to disillusion her.

While Mona sliced her croissant into even pieces, Almeida smiled and said nothing, as if changing a name could bring about instant improvement in life and straightening pictures in public places was a natural and useful thing to do.

"Yesterday it was the bank," Mona said. "The day before that, the Archer Gallery in Yorkville. I only touched the frame and an alarm went off. You'd think that would've stopped me—being regarded as a thief."

"Any particular pictures?"

"I see where you're going with this."

Almeida had only posed the question out of curiosity. She was glad when Mona went on without asking her to name her destination.

"You're saying are there men in the pictures? Do any of the men look like him? I have looked at them and seen no relevance. I've looked at the patterns and colours. There is nothing that has any connection to him. They can be scenes or ships or abstracts. But what I'm afraid of, Almeida, is that I'll start next on furniture. I am unable to stop myself."

"My husband has a similar problem," Almeida said.

"Your husband straightens pictures?"

"He was, is, a wood-carver. He didn't know how to stop either."

"Chainsaw art?"

"Oh my! Thank goodness no." Almeida lost herself for a moment in an Easter Island forest of heads, her own young self looming up from the ground every way she turned. "Just a chisel."

"I know that I could easily become obsessive. What shall I do?"

"Perhaps you could straighten things right where you work instead of in other places." It was the only advice Almeida could think of to offer.

At their next meeting Mona sat down in the booth, squared her place-mat with the table edge, put the salt and pepper and sauce exactly in the centre of the table, and said, "I left the house this morning without looking back. That's a sign of improvement, isn't it Almeida?"

Almeida nodded.

"It's a matter of understanding why. There is always a first cause. I went back to work but after I'd moved the water cooler and put all the files in order my secretary threatened to quit. When I tried to align the computers, I loosened some connection or other. Information was lost. They told me to take time out. And I have clients coming in to discuss their portfolios. I have to be there."

"I think there are groups," Almeida said. There had to be. There were groups to help gamblers, drinkers, smokers, why not the world's neatness freaks. And immediately she apologised silently for having used the word *freaks* even in her head.

"I am not going to stand up in front of a bunch of total strangers and say, My name is Mona and I straighten pictures in public places. I have to find the source myself. And the cure."

What was it in a person's life or mind that made a hobby, a little pastime, become the major event, as with Joe? Or made someone like Mona try to set straight the entire world? Joe had scarcely stopped to eat and certainly not to talk or go with her to a movie or do any other thing at all. It was as if he had to fill the entire space and block out everything and everybody.

"What about the children?"

"Zach and Emmie. They complained about me putting their posters in alignment, tidying their drawers. Don't most mothers do that?"

Only those with tons of time, Almeida thought.

"They've told her, that woman. Now they all, all four of them, think I'm weird. Probably they tell their neighbours and the kids tell their friends."

"You are their mother," Almeida said because it was all she could think of to say.

She promised to have coffee with Mona again the following week after their stint in the church basement, and hoped that between now and then some glimmer of inspiration would enable her to help this very clever child.

She couldn't get out of her mind an image of Mona squaring tables in cafés, sofas in hotel lobbies, organising the people in movie line-ups according to height.

She mentioned Mona to Jean but Jean treated her story with impatience. Dwayne was back. There was conflict. Mona was a stranger. Almeida should put her back where she'd found her. She was obviously a fruitcake, a fruitcake who could afford a psychiatrist. Uneducated advice was dangerous and could only make matters worse. Thinking of the lost information in Mona's workplace, Almeida didn't argue.

On her way home, she went to the library. The key, if there was one, had to be there.

Wandering among the stacks, she was overwhelmed by the amount of stuff she couldn't ever read or understand. She didn't know where to begin. She ricocheted from one shelf to another. The librarian glanced at her

[76]

as if she was the sort of person who would tear recipes out of magazines and pages from travel books.

She moved quickly into Romance to search for clues. She took a book from the shelf and flicked the pages. When had love ever had anything to do with 'scudding clouds' or a 'face against her firm ripe flesh'? And what did she, Almeida Kerwell, know about it anyway? Ivar was a mistake. The man in Vancouver? Standing on the Sea Wall, ten years younger, single, well on her own anyway, the man called—what was he called? It began with a hard sound like a stone. The sea was licking at the stones like a cat licking milk from a saucer and Keith, his name was Keith, had said to her, "We could have a cosy time together you and me." And that was as near as she'd come to romance in a good long time.

She turned left and found reality. Psychology. Compulsion. "I approached this subject with trepidation," the author with a dozen letters after his name, had written. What chance was there then for her? "Every compulsion is an act of terror," he stated. "Compulsion can occur during a contented period of life." And then, "Liz felt she was undeserving." Confused and afraid, Almeida went out into the street.

The city changed overnight from chilly spring to steamy summer. She woke up in a sweat. Joe called to say he had bought an air conditioner, secondhand but in full working order.

"Good for you," she said cruelly then asked him how he was and listened as he told her his cold was better but didn't wait for him to say, *I am lonely, deserted, bereft.* She didn't ask him why, when he was retired he couldn't, like other men, take up a hobby in a rational way and leave part of the day for companionship, that supposed benefit of the twilight years. In moments of depression she could only think it was she herself who had driven him to bury his head in sawdust.

The temperature was 27 degrees Celsius and the last thing Almeida wanted to do was sit with Mona and listen to her list of woes. It was in her mind to tell her to get a life, to consider the people who through no fault of their own had to line up for boxes of food, maybe not even food they particularly liked. She wanted to boast about Harriet, whose life was devoted to saving the desperate.

She had time to spare and headed for the cool library again. She found *Treasures of the Louvre* and took the heavy book over to a table. For ten minutes, she sat and stared at the most famous painting in the world.

So, Almeida said to the face, *why are you smiling, Mona?* She looked until the eyes looked back at her. Who was she? There were several candidates. No one knew now whether it was the woman whose name really was Mona-Lisa, or an Isabella, or a Constanza, or a self-portrait of Leonardo. The gown was gathered low on her bosom with a kind of smocking stitch. The hair was arranged in today's young blown-casual style. The mouth appeared to twitch.

Scholars were still trying to figure out this woman's state of mind. For nearly five hundred years, she had looked quietly out at the world, keeping her thoughts to herself. Those eyes, the faint curve of the lips, were the expression of a woman who knew more than she was ever going to tell. It was no use asking.

Almeida hurried along to the café, running encouraging phrases through her mind, words to cheer her young friend on. *Steven will come to realise he's made a mistake.* A hopeful lie. *Get yourself a lover.* For heaven's sake, Almeida!

But here was Mona coming towards her smiling, with a gift in her hand.

"I want to thank you," she said.

Almeida wanted to ask what for but she sensed the answer coming so she waited.

"Almeida, you have made all the difference. It was what you said. I realised that some things in life are immutable and therefore it's no use reacting with impatience. I was banging my head on the metaphorical wall. I stopped sitting by the phone. I went back to the office and the only things I straightened were the papers on my desk. I let the kids watch TV and eat chips. Steven is unhappy. And it's all due to you. I'll always be grateful."

"I only," Almeida began but stopped because she couldn't think what she had 'only' done.

Mona, obviously too busy to have coffee, gave her the gift and kissed her and said, "I'd like to think we might meet now and then."

"Will you change your name back?"

Mona shook her head. To change her name back would be to tempt fate, to tell the world that she had expectations. This way, she could hang on to her secrets, hold the world at arm's-length and continue to smile a little.

Almeida sat by herself in the café. It was weird, the way when you thought you were doing one kind of good deed, you were, without knowing it, doing another. It certainly made doing good by stealth a whole lot easier.

[79]

She took the shiny gold gift wrap off the package Mona had given her. Inside was a tiny, expensive bottle of Envy. Hardly the scent for a woman of her age to wear in the morning. It would end up in Geraldine's Christmas stocking.

She went outside again into the heat and walked slowly along Dundas. She had to do something before another sleepless summer night drove her back to Joe and the air conditioner. She stopped at Wah Lee's stall and bought a taro root. Its mottled brown and beige skin reminded her of certain seashells, the bark of birch trees. Even if she never figured out how to cook it, she could keep it as an ornament to remind her of Mona. She held the root in her hand, it was light, it had its own beauty and for her it was a little step into another world.

Becoming Chinese

Almeida woke up that Monday morning wishing she was Chinese. She wanted to be small, delicate, and have thick, shiny black hair. She wanted to have come from Sichuan province and speak a difficult language and believe that she could have another chance at life. She wanted to be the best student in her calligraphy class.

It wasn't a dream that made her wish for oriental features but Jean's comment the day before about the passengers on the Dundas streetcar. "Have you noticed," Jean had said, "how exotic-looking, how lovely, all the people are except for us. Some of them are brown, some are a delicate taupe. Our skin is the colour of worms, our hair looks as though it's been in the dryer and . . ."

And?

"And there is no health in us," Almeida had responded remembering an old prayer she'd recited often in church as a child, wondering all the while why this had to be said when most of the congregation were clearly as fit as fleas.

She stared into the bathroom mirror, hesitating to put on either the light or her glasses. They had set the clocks back. Daylight was increasing. Spring would very soon show up all her wrinkles and the mark on her cheek that she feared was cancer but was afraid to ask the doctor about. Her hair looked like a bad wig sprouting out in all directions, undecided whether to be grey or brown.

She put on her navy two-piece and decided to be late for work. They were still, behind her back, sniggering about Ivar. Only Andra in Personnel who after all was trained to deal with people, had complimented Almeida on the way she'd helped him with his English. "He left here much more fluent than he arrived," she'd said last week. "Thanks to you, Almeida." If there was sarcasm in her tone, Almeida had chosen to ignore it.

She had only ten more working days to go anyway. Even Combined Charities was down-sizing. And without putting it into so many words, Andra had suggested that now she was over sixty, it was time for Almeida to take up a more leisurely life. To get involved in nice pursuits like bridge and writing the family history. She should take satisfaction in performing charitable deeds for nothing.

"Leisure," Almeida said to Jean next day, "is a frightening word. It means time out. It means not having enough money to travel, sliding down the slope to darkness. Leisure is having time to tell the children whether I want to be cremated or buried. For working on the will. My grandmother knew all about leisure. She stitched forty-three

Christmas tree quilts in her last ten years and when she died she was knitting a toilet roll cover. I could easily sink into despair."

She saw Jean's look and moved on to a better topic. Jean had been at leisure for several years and looking after her useless and almost middle-aged son couldn't have been as fulfilling as she liked to make out. Her friends referred to her behind her back as a martyr and sometimes as stupid for not having kicked the vegetable out into the street years ago.

To make up for her lack of tact, Almeida asked after Dwayne and let Jean tell her of his latest attempt to find work.

Walking up Spadina afterwards, Almeida began to think more about the Chinese approach to life and death. Why was it possible to consider a heaven and a hell and not, as millions of the earth's inhabitants did, the idea of a future life in a new role?

This thought was not flippant. It wasn't, In my next life I'll be a thin blonde, but rather, I'll be a Chinese woman and leave my peasant roots and become a leader. An organiser of the down-trodden. Or, I will take the totally spiritual path and learn to exist without material goods.

She skipped her next lunch date with Jean and went to the library. There was a great deal to know. At the farewell-and-thank-you party in the office, her head was so full of new thoughts that she scarcely noticed how celebratory the event was. They were happy to be able to fill her space with someone they thought was more efficient; she was happy to be free. Andra told her to make sure she had three meals a day and kept up her exercise routine. She gave her a pamphlet containing this and other good advice. Almeida threw it into the trash can on the way home.

Jean called her to say that if she needed company now in this traumatic time, she would come and spend the day. Almeida said she wanted to go through the separation process alone. Jean mentioned Joe. Almeida said there was someone at the door and hung up.

The Chinese calligraphy instructor growled at the thinness of her down strokes. Wen Lo, she sensed, was not a happy man. Teaching these worm-coloured people fragments of his culture was perhaps not his idea of a life and she wondered what he might have previously been. And did he look forward to a reincarnation in which he would be a mountaineer, a cowboy, a true artist? That philosophy gave a person immense scope but she was not foolish enough to think she would have a choice in the matter. Like much else in life it was most likely a lottery. Worse still, it might be that one became in the next life what one deserved according to one's behaviour in this.

The teacher shooed them out of the room early. He looked tired and coughed frequently. Perhaps he hated them all for trying to attach themselves to a civilisation going back five thousand years of which they understood nothing but what they could see with their misshapen eyes.

She stopped in at the Hunan Garden for green tea and almond cookies.

And there, peering into the window, was Joe.

Don't run away was a precept she had been taught early on by a father who had faced down a moose bare-handed, so he said. And who had caught many a deer in his headlights and not allowed their pleading eyes to stop him in his tracks.

"Joe," she said.

"Come back to me," he pleaded fish-like through the glass with the streetcar rattling along Dundas Street behind him.

"Drop dead," she replied.

In the park behind the Gallery most mornings, old people were stretching out their arms and legs in a pantomime of slow aggression. She often stopped to watch. She liked the look of it. It would help keep her concentration and prevent her joints from seizing up.

When she finally got to the Tai Chi class, she was three weeks late and the instructor, a beautiful dark-haired woman in a white robe, waved her to a place and watched as she copied the moves of the person beside her. Almeida realised she had a long way to go before she could *grasp the bird's tail* in a truly Chinese way.

She mentioned something of her new life to Jean and Jean said, "Fortune cookies aren't mottoes to live by. They're the joke of a moment."

Dwayne had left, finally, just after his thirty-third birthday. Jean's very late empty nest syndrome was making her sharp, almost bitter. Her oatmeal cookies had become even harder. Her usual sympathy was lacking. She told Almeida she needed her head read.

In the classroom, Almeida found the overlaid glyphs very difficult to imitate. She wanted to work on the *Ling chih*, the Plant of Immortality, but Wen Lo set her on to the much simpler *Grain Measure*. With no idea of what she was putting on the paper, she feared that she was being crude. Wen Lo looked at her work and sighed his patient sigh.

As if he spent his life walking up and down Dundas Street in hopes of seeing her, Joe appeared at the teashop window again. It was raining a heavy April rain. She asked for another cup and beckoned him inside.

Joe said, "I've sold my chisels, I can get a new mortgage on the house, cut into my RRSP. Look."

He pushed a travel agent's brochure across the table. "Shanghai," he said.

"'It took more than one man to change my name to Shanghai Lily,'" Almeida quoted before she could stop herself. Decades ago they had fallen into the habit of trading lines from the movies for fun. James Cagney was Joe's specialty. The sexy superstars were hers. But that was when they were young. He was serious now.

"Beijing," he went on, "Xi'an. Yunan. The Yangtse River. Inner Mongolia. Sixty-three days. Fully escorted."

Green rivers and mountains and a sea of people looped through Almeida's mind. She sat back astonished not only at the itinerary but at the price.

Finally she pushed the shiny booklet back across the table. "Might as well be Mars," she told him.

She looked at his face and saw that she had been unkind. She tasted the tea and wished it was Orange Pekoe. Too much Tai Chi, too much awareness that she would never be able to make all the symbols of the mandarin lexicon were making her mean. The trap-door finally opened and let into her consciousness the fact that she had been put out to grass. She had had a working life: twelve years with Dr. Singh; nineteen years in the accounts department at Eatons; a couple of years at Combined Charities. And here she was, out to grass like an old horse. Joe knew. He knew how she had loved to travel. He saw that she was looking into a long vacant space, just as he had done. He had filled his time with carving heads. Now to help her, he was offering a whole subcontinent.

"It's a lovely idea," she said. "Thank you, Joe."

"If you're learning to be Chinese," he said, "you might as well see where they live."

"How long could you afford to live if you spent all that money?"

He hesitated a moment before holding up his right hand with the fingers spread out.

She shook her head. It was just like him to go barrelling on without any sense of proportion. Not for him the idea of making one or two or even three carvings of her head. He had made dozens. Filled the house. Till she'd had to leave, overwhelmed by images of herself.

"We could both go entirely broke," she said.

She pictured them landing on Geraldine's doorstep in a few year's time. All their household goods dumped on the sidewalk by a mover they hadn't been able to pay.

We're here, sweetheart, they would say in chorus in their old croaky voices.

The look on Geraldine's face in that scene wasn't hard to imagine. She loved her parents but couldn't stand them for more than one day, two at a stretch. Having discussed this with other parents, Almeida had come to see that a day was quite a long time and that she and Joe must after all have done something right.

"Entirely broke," she repeated.

Joe put the brochure back in his pocket and sipped the tea, pulling a face.

"We'd take our own teabags," he said.

"I was on the streetcar," Jean said, "and I saw you walking along with your nose in the air. What were you doing?"

"Inhaling," Almeida answered.

"I usually breathe through my mouth when I walk along past all that cabbage."

"Smells are as much a part of a culture as its music."

"Ah," Jean said.

"*Gwen chu chiu*," Almeida replied.

"Why can't you learn French like everyone else?"

"Chinese music is exacting."

She had spent the evening before playing her new cassette of Chinese opera, trying to get used to the sounds. Even Wagner seemed more listener-friendly. Even hip-hop. It would take time and devotion.

"You'd be better off going back to Joe."

"If you're so keen, why don't you move in with him."

Almeida saw at once that she had been mean again and said she was sorry.

"I've just finally got the house to myself," Jean said.

"Well you know what it's like then."

Joe met her at the teashop again with a different and much cheaper plan. Three days in Beijing, two days in Xi'an, a tour of Shanghai, a stopover in Korea and back home by the following Friday.

"And when we get back?"

She knew he was about to suggest that she sublet her apartment, better still give it up, better even yet, move back to the house with him. She knew collusion when she fell over it. Jean and Joe. She could just see them wondering together what poor Almeida would do now with all her free time.

She looked at her ex-husband. A lonely man. Was it possible that if there was another life beyond this, they would return to earth as a pair of oxen harnessed together under a wooden yoke, ploughing fields in a remote Chinese province till they dropped? She said no to him as gently as she could.

Wen Lo invited her to his home. She was proud and pleased that of the fourteen students in his class, she was the chosen one. She looked around his living room. So quiet. So neat. Nothing unnecessary. And on the wall, two paintings. One of a bare tree against a pink background, lacy and delicate. She was drawn to the other, larger picture. The buildings, red with black roofs, were tilted this way and that as if they were made of flexible material. Tall buildings built of brick and stone but distorted, not made to last, shaken perhaps by an earthquake, pagoda-like shapes seen through a thin film of soft white petals.

"Beijing?" she asked.

"Ottawa in winter," Wen Lo answered as if it should be obvious.

She sat down opposite him and drank the tea he gave her. Took the soft cookies and ate them as if they might help her to be a better student. He talked to her about his home in China and suggested she give up calligraphy and take painting lessons. There were moments of silence. Someone was moving around in another room. She felt suspended in time. When she left, Wen Lo gave her a coloured fan.

She called Joe when she got home and met him next day at Second Cup on Bloor Street.

"I'll come to Shanghai," she said. "I'd like to see the Great Wall and the terra-cotta army if we can afford it. I'll pay my way."

He looked at her. She looked at him, the aging image of the boy. Hair almost gone, a grey fringe round the back of his head, his complexion still clear, his eyes always with that enquiring sharpness in them.

He said quickly as if she might instantly change her mind, "You'd better get some shots and insurance and make sure your passport's up-to-date."

"What will the weather be like?"

"The annual average summer temperature in China is twenty degrees Celsius. And by the way, Almeida, maybe when we get back—"

"*Ta ma da*," she said. And without understanding a syllable of the language he knew when not to push his luck.

He was not stupid. There was more to being Joe than a bunch of chisels and filling in the time with patient reproduction and the air with sawdust.

"There is more to being me," she said to him, "than worm-pink skin and fried hair."

"Your hair's fine," he said. "There's nothing wrong with your hair. It was pretty hard though to do in wood. It flew off in chips. Your hair, when it was long—" He stopped himself in mid-memory and began to drink his coffee.

"I'll bring a silk shirt back for each of the girls," she said, making lists in her mind.

"What made you change your mind?" Joe asked.

"Ottawa."

"The government!"

"There's more to being Chinese than making a few brushstrokes," Almeida replied.

She decided to walk home. Along Dundas. Through Chinatown. It was going to be a long march towards reality.

Beyond This Point

"You had the tickets when we left, honey!" The angry man at the next table was shouting loudly enough to be heard in Hamilton.

Almeida looking round knew that her glittering silk blouse was the wrong thing to wear for this occasion. It had appeared brownish gold in the store but here under the light she felt as if her upper body had turned into a nuclear pumpkin, glowing, giving off heat. And surely it would signal to Joe that she was ready to have sex with him as soon as they were alone in a room with a double bed. They were going to have to share on account of the heavy single supplement. He'd said nothing about it but was capable of being cagy. His father had spent his salary at the poker table.

"No! You had them last," the angry man's partner replied.

Joe had simply said "Wow!" when she'd taken off her jacket. She would have liked to tell him that she wanted to shine and that was why she'd worn her silver earrings and the bracelet to match, and the opal brooch which was her mother's only legacy. But it wasn't true. It was more like dressing up to go the scaffold. A fine show in the face of peril.

All the others at the table appeared, at first look, to be wearing cream and beige. They blended into a blur of vanilla. Talking in soft colourless phrases, the other four looked serious enough to cry. They were leaning in towards her and Joe as if to hold them, keep them in their place.

"I gave the tickets to you," the man said even louder.

A few years ago, Joe would have looked at her blouse and said, "The Christmas Tree's thataway," or some such smartass thing. The fact that now he only said "Wow!" meant they'd been apart for so long he was afraid to speak his mind.

"Hey! Loaded for bear, Almeida," Melvin said to her in his crass way, walking across to the table, tripping over Joe's flight bag *en route*. He gave Almeida a kiss before he sat down. He was late. "Something came up at the office." Most likely a couple of drinks in a bar. "Don't you look great. All set for the big trip. Second honeymoon, eh Joe."

Almeida hoped that in China she would learn some non-interfering way of telling Geraldine that there could be life after Melvin.

"What are we having? Wine to bless the travellers. Must have wine."

"You can't get wine in here, Mel. It's only a cafeteria," Geraldine told him.

[93]

"What kind of party is this?"

No one answered him because none of them were sure whether it was right to celebrate when two older people were about to set out on a journey to the unknown.

Jean had chosen a sandwich so big she could hardly get her mouth round it. She nibbled the edges, glanced at Almeida's daughters, watched her own son, Dwayne, eating his hot dog. Harriet was lifting the lettuce on her plate with her fork, looking under the leaves, prospecting for caterpillars the way she'd done since she was five.

Melvin said, "I was on this plane once when the attendant went crazy, started rushing up and down the aisle handing out those little packages of peanuts and cookies so fast it was a joke. In the end she was throwing them, shouting 'Catch you bastards, catch!' As if we were seals or something."

Geraldine said, "Melvin, you told us that a dozen times."

Not put down, Melvin went on, "Well it was weird. They took her off the plane in Edmonton."

Dwayne had to say, "Best place for her," and then laugh so loudly that tired people walking by, dragging their luggage, turned and shook their heads, and the couple at the next table stopped arguing for a moment.

Gerry and Harriet and Jean. Two daughters and a friend. All three nervous. All three worried because she and Joe were setting off for a place perceived as unknown! A place that had been civilised for about four thousand years before there was Europe, and still they called it unknown. She wished she was back in the classroom with Wen Lo's patient friend, learning to paint a tree.

"Who are the barbarians?" she asked and when they looked at her, knew she had spoken her thought aloud.

"You'll find out," Dwayne said.

Melvin said, "So it's Vancouver, Hong Kong? And then into the great Republic, eh?"

And just by his saying it, it became real. Startled, Almeida retraced her steps. She'd left Joe on account of his hobby. Not the hobby itself but its proof that he had never accepted her current self, the older, mature version. Lived apart from him for twenty-three months. Decided she would not ever live with him again. So why, now, had she agreed to go on this long journey with him! Was it a kind of reward for him? Was it a last-chance trip? There were a million things she could be doing. Like playing cards with the old folk in the Lodge. Saying she was going to China had sounded like the worst excuse in the world. She would be written off, marked down as unhelpful. Gone to China indeed!

It wouldn't be difficult to get up and say she wasn't going; to return to the apartment and tell the two Chinese students she'd changed her mind and they must find somewhere else to stay. In the morning, she'd walk as usual to the corner for her newspaper. Come back and turn on the radio, have coffee, consider the day ahead. One of her father's often repeated maxims was, *only a fool never changes his mind.* It was about the only thing she could remember him saying that didn't have to do with the killing and skinning of wild animals.

She went on listening to the voices around her for clues and signs. At the next table, the man and woman were muttering, turning their flight bags inside out, books, socks, water bottles.

Harriet was saying, "Now if there's the slightest bit of trouble, you're to go to the nearest Canadian embassy and tell them who you are."

She handed her parents a wrapped gift each. They smiled at her and took the paper off. Joe folded the wrap neatly and put it on the table then looked with delight at the pair of pocket-sized binoculars. Almeida fought back tears when she saw the coloured plastic bag with its collection of remedies, something for headache, for stomach upsets, for constipation, for purifying water. Even a little light for clipping onto a book so that she could read in the dark.

"There's nothing here for homesickness," Almeida said and reached out to Harriet in a grateful way.

Harriet did smile. She understood her mother's jokes once in a while. She clasped her mother's hand and said, "I hope you have a great time."

"I gave the tickets to you. I remember. They were on the dresser and I picked them up and you took them." The distraught couple stood up and began to walk away.

Almeida wanted to run after them and yell, "How would you like to go to China?"

But Jean was saying, "I saw a show on TV about the standing army. I wanted more than anything to go there and see them in the flesh. I mean in the clay. My flesh. Their clay. I'm gibbering. Sorry."

Dwayne said, "By going there you're telling them you approve of repression and torture."

Almeida felt that in a way Dwayne was right but she saw herself and Joe buying a silk shirt from a stall, paying a fair price to someone who desperately needed the money. There had to be, in a country like China, millions of ordinary people who would smile back at her when she smiled at them. Who would see her and Joe as they were. Two other human runners in the same race but with a different set of rules.

Harriet said, "Let them alone, Dwayne."

And Jean asked him to get her another cup of coffee.

Almeida watched Joe's face. He'd wanted no farewells, wanted only to be dropped off at the check-in desk, waved to, and left alone with her. He was quiet, waiting like an animal to pounce on the moment when he could rightly get up and say, *It's time we went.*

"You are an idiot!" The ticketless pair rushed by in the other direction this time, back towards the airline counters, perhaps to have their problem solved.

Geraldine was saying, "Now mother. Don't go spending your money on bits of this and that. Get yourself a silk suit. Or one of those nice robes with embroidery on."

Almeida nodded. Geraldine had told her in this way, what she herself would like if Almeida could afford it and Almeida took note. Geraldine's days couldn't be wonderful. Melvin was Melvin. Sharon and Tyler were growing impatient and would leave home soon. It was the way of things.

She could easily lean across the table now and say to Joe that she shouldn't leave Geraldine in this state. Geraldine was a mere child of nearly thirty-nine who needed a mother's support.

"And what about Jean?" she might say. Jean has been my friend all these years. She has need of me. Her son is going crazy and draining her of life.

At a table across the aisle, two adults and three small children were eating in a sleepy, trance-like way as if their molecules were being transported even as they sat there and they would wake up reassembled in Hawaii. The littlest one was no bigger than the child who had been allowed to fly a plane because she wanted to. And had died. Almeida hadn't been able to get that out of her mind. That parents would allow a child to do something so plainly dangerous, in the name of freedom.

"I hope you've been practising with your chopsticks," Dwayne said and laughed again. His new job had lasted only three months.

Air Canada flight number 097 to Vancouver and Hong Kong is now ready for boarding. Please proceed...

Almeida panicked. Agreeing to go on this trip had been the madness of a moment, a decision made under the influence of April rain and scented tea. The money could be used in a variety of ways, some of it given to charity, some of it spent on better clothes, a new chair. She could go home at once. Fall asleep in her own bed to the sound of the streetcar creaking its way up the hill towards Roncesvalles.

Geraldine was itching, Almeida knew, to raise her water glass and toast her parents coming back together. But she wanted them together here, in Toronto, their right place. At home. She'd given Almeida a bottle of cologne to keep her fresh on the journey, and Joe a book about the Long March but she still couldn't believe they would go. She leaned to her mother now and whispered in her ear, "There's cancellation insurance. You'd get most of the money back."

"Most of the money?" Almeida asked.

"It's such a long way."

"I'll bring you something."

"Just take care of yourselves."

"We should be on our way," Joe said.

But still they all stayed as if they couldn't decide who was meant to be leaving. Or who had invited them. Or why they were all sitting round a plastic-topped table, eating food off trays. Or how they could escape from this facsimile of hell full of weary people, edgy people, people rushing, waiting, not a single one of all these hundreds at ease. Barring, apparently, Melvin who now said, "There's a little place I've heard of in Shanghai, Joe, if you can get away by yourself."

Joe replied, "Melvin, you and me, we don't travel the same way."

Harriet turned to Joe and said, "It's not too late, Dad."

Harriet for whom trips to Europe, South America, Indonesia were a routine part of her job, was upset. Her lip was quivering as it had when, as a child, she'd felt unfairly treated. "At your age."

"We're not as old as you think," Joe told her.

Dwayne said, "The trouble with the economy is too many people are spending their vacation dollars abroad."

Jean pushed aside the remains of her plate with the frayed club sandwich on it. She took a deep breath before she spoke.

"The world is a big place," she said, "and I'd like if I had the chance, to see as much of it as I possibly could while I can still move around. If I could afford it, I'd go to the Hindu Kush. It's always appealed to me. I'd go to Tierra del Fuego and Peru. And ride a mule down the Grand Canyon. Muskoka is all right but it has no strangeness. And television is unsatisfactory."

Almeida got up from her place and went to hug her friend. It was an awkward embrace. She saw, did Almeida, that this was a selfish trip. They could have taken a shorter journey and included Jean. Three of them perhaps toiling up the steps of the pyramid in Mexico City. One of them having a heart attack in all that heat and rolling all the way to the bottom, knocking down other tourists like ninepins.

Guilt was being thrust at her from all sides. She saw now no reason for the journey except that when Joe had suggested it, she'd been caught up in the very idea of China. The picture she'd seen in Wen Lo's home, pagodas and petals, painted with oriental delicacy but called *Ottawa in Winter*, had sideswiped her perspective. She'd gone right out and told Joe that yes, yes indeed, she would come with him. And now her conscience was rearing up like a frightened horse. Was she letting down her friend, failing her children, spending money she could have left to her grandchildren? She stood up straight, ready to run away. She wanted to get her ticket from Joe that very moment and tear it up, shred it, let it float here in the leftover coffee in all these cups. Or take the tickets and shout to this crowd like an auctioneer that the first bidder could have them. She glanced around, but the arguing couple had disappeared and none of the people at the other tables looked as if they would appreciate a sudden change in destination.

She heard Joe's voice saying, "Well, it's time we were on our way," and searched around for the nearest red Exit sign.

Joe thought perhaps it was always like this. Life. People

[100]

going, other people seeing them off, out of this world to another. He was pleased now that Geraldine had come though he could see she was getting on her mother's nerves. He shuddered when he heard her say, "Just because it's prepaid you don't have to keep on. What if you get sick so far away and have no insurance and go into a Chinese hospital?"

It was Melvin who saved him then. Melvin cried out, "Gerry! They should've called you Jeremiah. Leave them be. So what if they drop dead over there. They'll be having a great time. In the midst of life and all that. New experiences."

Geraldine began to dab at her eyes. Dwayne laughed.

Almeida said, "Well it would be a new experience for one of us, travelling home with a coffin."

Joe said, "I'd have no problem being buried in China."

Harriet smiled a tight smile and did not say that no doubt she would be the one who would have to come to their rescue.

Jean was glancing about like a caged animal.

Joe sensed the desperation in the air and picked up his flight bag. Almeida had made no objection when he'd booked a longer trip for them. A compromise. "You can't do China in ten days. It's an insult to a country." And she had agreed. She'd always had that quality of fairness which he liked. But she might, any moment, turn and bolt if they didn't move right away.

Once they were on the plane he would tell her about the bonfire. Or maybe he'd wait till they were sitting in a real Chinese restaurant struggling to eat rice with chopsticks. "I've burnt all the heads except the last few," he would say. "You are the only real Almeida."

Geraldine said "Come back safely."

Joe said more firmly, "Time to go." He had to get Almeida away from the kids, from Jean, Dwayne, from their disbelieving faces, their mouths in the shapes of all five vowels, their staring eyes. All of them were expecting any moment that he and Almeida would turn back, hand over their tickets, say sorry for being presumptuous, for even daring to think that they of all people might set out across the world to a place so strange that aside from pictures on TV it was damn near unimaginable.

He stood back to watch Almeida being hugged by Jean as if she was never to return although he'd heard himself repeating "totally escorted" several times and especially loudly after Melvin had told about his friend's arm being slashed to ribbons for the sake of a cheap watch.

Harriet came close to hug him and whisper, "Have a great time, Dad. Love you." And let him go.

"See you next month, honey," he answered.

He took Almeida's arm and led her towards the sign that said, Passengers Only Beyond This Point. She was looking down and saying nothing. Her feet seemed reluctant. But back there in the café, an hour ago, as soon as he'd helped her off with her jacket, he'd read her bold blouse as a pledge, a hat thrown into the ring of chance.

"Harriet," she called over her shoulder, as though there was one last thing to say, but a group of travellers got in the way. There was a barrier between them now.

"Boarding passes, please."

She put her flight bag on the conveyor belt, and the security person beckoned her to go through the arch.

[102]

Joe felt a thrill run through him like an electric charge. There was adventure ahead. They were not too old. They were launching themselves like a couple of rockets towards an unknown space. As he walked through the metal detector, Almeida looked beyond him as if seeking a way to escape. Then she smiled at him, and he knew she was with him at last.

Melvin and Geraldine

On their way back from the airport Gerry said, "I guess they'll be OK."

Melvin replied, "They'll be fine."

"I should be driving."

"I'm OK. How did it go today?"

"I got a real offer."

"I hope it goes through."

Gerry looked at her husband, the marks on his face, the soft cheeks mottled now with bristles, dark lines under the eyes, and knew something was wrong. His usual way was to treat her recent foray into real estate as a hobby, a kind of needlework to keep her hands occupied. Something at which she could never succeed. The very fact of him asking, asking without a joke or the hint of a laugh, meant he was troubled.

"Did you have a good day?" she asked him in her turn.

"No," he replied. "No."

And the word had a warning in it. Yield, like the road sign. Wait. Do not proceed without a green light. Change direction. The man who normally talked a blue streak said nothing more.

It was his job! How long could a man like him keep a position in which tact and gentle persuasion were basic requirements. He sometimes behaved like the archetype used car salesman, a cartoon figure with his back-slapping manner, his quick and awful one-liners, his habit of drinking three rye-and-waters before dinner. No wonder he wanted to know if she'd made a sale. She'd been promoted overnight to major breadwinner.

"You want to talk, Mel?"

"Not right now."

He'd been to the doctor and learned he had inoperable prostate cancer! He was choosing the moment to tell her. The very fact that he could be present and laughing at the airport showed his courage. That same courage had made him leap into the water when Sharon was caught in the whirlpool at the base of the natural waterslide. Even though he could hardly swim and both of them had to be rescued. He would go through to the end with commendable bravery, reducing her and all those around to weeping admiration. *After a brave fight.*

"You feeling OK?"

"Fine."

Geraldine began to wish they'd brought Harriet home with them for the night so that there would be no need for her to wallow in this pit of speculation. Melvin would be teasing Harriet about her precarious life. Harriet would be paying him back in kind. He admired her.

And maybe wished that his wife were more like her sister, bold and independent. Harriet's life contained no permanent man, no ties, and made Geraldine shriek within herself. And left her with the big question: Was what Harriet did more important than her own dedication to bringing up the kids, looking after this man who now, sitting beside her, seemed for the first time in eighteen years of marriage to have lost his tongue? And there was another question that only came to her in the night. Did she love Harriet as a sister should when envy stood between them like a green unclimbable wall?

They'd be home in another ten minutes at the speed he was driving with lights flashing down on them, the wet road ahead shining in the dark. He'd pour himself a drink. Pour one for her. And then he'd say, *I guess it's over, Gerry. I'm moving my stuff out tomorrow.*

And you waited till my parents have left the country! She tried in her mind for the right tone of voice, whether to shriek the words out or utter them with deadly quiet. His reply: *I thought it best, didn't want to upset them.* Her response: *And you didn't care about upsetting me? The kids?*

She glared at him. How could he, even he, play such a rotten trick? Was it the woman in the office? How commonplace. How stupidly ordinary. Fury rose up in her. That he could wait so deliberately until Mom and Dad had left for China, knowing she would be vulnerable, fearful for them. She wanted to hit him hard, push his head down onto the steering wheel and was amazed at her own violence. She guided her thoughts back to the discomfort of prostate cancer, the men-only disease. Perhaps it was that.

"You're quiet."

"Concentrating on the road."

He knew something about one of the kids. Sharon, with her changing body and difficult moods. They'd called him rather than her. Told him she'd run away with the middle-aged man who delivered pizza. Not that, no. She could rule that out. He wouldn't have remained cheerful through that. Even if he'd been able to maintain his facade through that awkward hour in the airport cafeteria, he would have yelled at her as soon as they got to the parking lot. Told her it was her fault for not being there, for thinking she could compete in the business world when she should've been at home, keeping watch.

Tyler! Not his favourite child but all the same a source of pride. *Doesn't play football but knows more about computers than Bill Gates.* Their son the genius! If Tyler had ridden his bike into a wall, he would have said something. Told her by now. Been in his own way kind.

"Kind of a house did you get the offer on?"

"The one I told you. Grove Street. Three beds, two baths, den in the basement could be rented."

"God! I do not think," he began and then stopped. What! What do you not think! she screamed, mute.

"When we get home," she said but before she could finish, he pushed the button on the radio and a voice invaded the car. "This morning in Shanghai students rioted in the street and the police fought back with tear gas and rubber bullets injuring several."

"Oh," she said.

"They won't let them anywhere dangerous," he said. "It's a tour. It's not good for business, any of them get whacked."

As many words nearly as he'd said the whole drive. Words to reassure. Kindness always lurking under the heavy humour, the pat on the behind he'd had to learn not to do.

He slowed down to turn in the driveway. With her Dad's help they'd been able to buy this desirable two-storey, large lot, four-bedroom, basement with potential, ten years ago. And had paid the loan back ahead of time. Not many vacations. Fewer clothes than she would've liked. But it was all theirs. Their own house. Home. All, at one time, she'd ever wanted.

Inside, she hung up her raincoat, watched him lock the door.

"Sharon!" he called out.

"Fine, Dad," came the reply. "Did they get off all right?"

"Sure. Skipped off like two kids."

Tyler was in the living room watching TV.

"Time for bed."

"I'm going." The boy kissed his mother and nodded at his father, leaving the room quickly as if he could sense pent-up secrets waiting to be told.

Six thuds as he leapt up the stairs missing every other one. Geraldine counted the seconds till Sharon's usual cry, "Get out of here, Tyle!" and then turned to her husband.

"You didn't eat anything. Like a sandwich?"

"Got any cheese?"

He went to sit in the chair by the window looking out into the darkness as if it had answers for a man like him. Yesterday, she'd sighed for freedom. Today, she wanted to know what in the world had changed him into this moping hulk.

"I'll make you a snack and then we'll talk," she said, taking charge.

In the kitchen she surveyed their married life so far. The knife she spread the marge on the bread with was one of a set given them as a wedding gift. Finest stainless because she'd said she'd be too busy studying to polish silver. And when, eventually, she became a lawyer, they'd eat out, have food sent in. All that remained of that fine dream was the cutlery. She cut the low-fat mozzarella into thin slices and put it between two pieces of whole grain bread with lettuce and mayonnaise.

The plate was part of a set she'd bought in those brief months she lived on her own. Bright, yellow and green. A reminder of a narrow apartment, a poster size copy of Van Gogh's *Sunflowers*, and days of laughter. They'd lasted through time, these plates. She still liked them. She set the sandwich out on the white centre and for decoration sliced a couple of radishes and put them round the edge.

She hadn't asked what he wanted to drink. She sat down at the kitchen table, given to them by his parents, marked with the burn ring where, drunk, Mel had set down a sauce pan, the knife mark where Tyler had cut through an apple, wine glass stains.

The various options played through her mind. Melvin lying in a hospital bed attached to tubes. *Always loved you, Gerry.* Melvin walking furtively out of a hotel backdoor in the early morning leaving behind an exhausted young and lovely woman. Or, his money gone on drink, he sat homeless and hopeless outside a shelter, waiting for the doors to open. *Spare any change, lady?*

In the room, there, through the adjoining wall, lurked some monstrous being, a package of all the fears of her life made real.

One thing she hadn't allowed herself to consider. That Melvin had heard about Stephen. Only a coffee now and then. What's wrong with that! A bit of a sympathetic friendship. Did you ever, till today, ask about my work, seriously? Stephen talks to me. He asks what I feel. He thinks of me. Shut up, she said to herself. Shut up, you sound like a woman on a talk show. Pathetic! If he is about to say, *It's over, Gerry,* face up to it. A shock. A trauma. Get counselling. Live through it. Call Stephen.

Mother wouldn't be in the least surprised. Might even be delighted but would not say I-told-you-so. Mom's view of their marriage was only what she saw, Melvin at his worst, trying jovially to please. And her Dad, what did he think? He never said a wrong word, only now and then responded to Mel in a kind of admonishing way, taking Mel's jokes too seriously maybe. Like at the airport, when Mel suggested Dad might take off to some brothel. As if it was likely!

And there was Harriet. When they were kids, wet days, playing indoors at the adventure games Harriet invented, plays she wrote. Gerry was always the princess, the pretty one, everybody said so. Was that why Harriet had gone her way into desperate places? Driven off by her sister's better looks. Well Harriet had won in the exciting life stakes, that was for sure.

Upstairs the shower was running, running. Sharon, who combined her grandmother's fine features with Mel's strength, was washing away the grime of her part-time job at the gas station. Sharon, who wanted to be like Aunt Harriet. Sharon, who felt that her mother had not so far been a role model.

Geraldine wished again that Harriet was there, right there in the kitchen, drinking a glass of her favourite red wine. She saw Harriet's face, the look that meant, Get on with it, Gerry. She said aloud, "I'm leaving Melvin. Melvin is leaving me." What did the words mean? "Melvin is dying, Harriet." But Melvin was living. Melvin was in the living room dying for a sandwich. And Harriet was up in the air, on her way back to Ottawa.

With the weight of all the alternatives hanging round her, Geraldine went to her husband and offered the tray to him. She had put a cloth on the tray, a napkin folded beside it, and had poured him a glass of milk and cut him a slice of pumpkin cake for comfort.

"So what is it?" she asked.

She sat opposite him and waited.

He looked at the tray on his lap and at her.

"Your Mom and Dad," he answered.

"What!"

"Going off to China like that."

"You said yourself not to worry."

"I mean, Gerry, they're nearly seventy. Your Dad is over seventy."

"We can't do anything about it. They've gone."

"It's not that. Like I said when we were seeing them off, if they've got to die, dying doing something like that is a great way to go."

"Mel!"

"Your Dad agreed with me. He said he wouldn't mind if he had to be buried over there."

"What's gotten into you?"

"Look, Gerry. There they are, old, taking a great step which they can hardly afford. It's a risk, a kind of gamble."

"I'm sure Dad figured it out to the last penny."

"What I want to know is, in another twenty-five years, you and me, Gerry? Will we be going to China? That's what I'm asking."

There were tears in his eyes. Tears in the eyes of her used-car salesman turned insurance-broker husband. If it was a trick, she thought, it was a damn good one. She went close to him, lifted the tray off his knees, put her arm round him and said as kindly as she could, "I don't know, Mel. But I tell you what, we'll start a trip-to-China account at the bank."

He looked at her as if he was about to apologise for his lost looks; his obtuse jokes; the day he'd come home late on her birthday carrying a bunch of broken flowers; the party he'd ruined by calling John Murphy a bogtrotter (a word he'd learned from an English colleague); the beer spilt on the piano. As if he was going to pour forth all the loving words she'd wanted to hear over the past few years. Or come to her and put his arms round her, become slim and sweet-smelling. Poetic even. Gently understanding. Quote her lines from the song that they'd called, in their young loving days, their own: "You are the lovely breath of springtime."

She held her breath and waited.

But all he said was, "Can we make it an Amazon account? I've always fancied the jungle." She had to let all the images in her mind drop away. It took a few moments. He was not leaving. He didn't have cancer. He hadn't heard about Stephen. All he wanted was time and life. Like everybody.

"The jungle? Of course," she said. "Sure we can. I'll go to the bank tomorrow. And if I sell the Grove Street place, we'll put half the commission in there. How's that?"

He wiped his eyes and sniffed.

"Thanks, Ger."

She put the tray back on his lap and sat beside him. Who knew if there'd be any jungle left in twenty years, or if she would want to go there if there was, or if she'd want to go anywhere at all with him. But there was no harm in calming a man's fears. At least for the time being.

Electric Blood

Tell me your favourite painting and I'll tell you who you are. But you've got to do it right away. No second thoughts so you can say Dürer's *Oswalt Krel* when really the one you like best is Rousseau's *Sleeping Gypsy*. My sister is thinking about me. I always know. The colours that come into my mind when I think of her are yellow and blue. The colours didn't come out well but it was one of my first attempts. A little old camera Dad gave me when I was twelve.

"I can't hold this up much longer. Besides I don't think you let it dry properly."

"Keep very still, Jess."

"What colour do you call this?"

"Used to be ultramarine. Now it's electric blood."

"Whatever, it's running down my face."

"Almost done. Don't talk. Please!"

We used to run through fields together but she got left behind because I could run faster. And people held her back. I paid no attention to her cries. Almeida and I don't see each other often but I've only got to look round and there she is. On my walls. I took that one at her wedding. She's leaning forward, smiling, trying to get me to catch a bouquet of freesia and carnations and I'm only waiting to get at the champagne and I dodge the flowers so that Mom catches them and bursts into tears. Her bridesmaids, tall, thin Helen and short, chunky Annie, don't look too thrilled either. Later at the reception, Joe comes up to me and from a corner of my right eye I can see Almeida willing him away from me. As if I'd run off with him straight from the wedding! She's too proud, old Almeida, to come and take his arm and say something like, there's someone here I'd like you to meet. Didn't have the social know-how. And I know any minute she's going to get mad and I can't help myself taking Joe's hand and walking a little way off with him. I want to catch the bridegroom, alone and pensive, on the greatest day of his life. So when I point the camera at him, I don't say, *Smile.*

Another picture I've kept all these years of that great day: Dad with his gun, pointing it at Joe pretending it was a shotgun wedding. Horrified looks from the guests. Nervous, fearful glances. Dad laughing. Joe about to wet his hired pants for Chrissake. I was the only one who ever understood Dad's sense of humour.

That picture of a tree has nothing to do with Almeida. And Simon isn't in it. I'm not in it. Just the tree. That was me in my terse phase. Every picture black and white and nothing unnecessary in any of them. And the tree was where we met; we were leaning against it when Simon told me he'd love me forever. A huge chestnut tree. Sold several copies of it. Never a problem with people saying what does this all mean. They figure it's all in the shadows, the light on the bark. But it's what you can't see in the picture that gives it its meaning.

"I need a drink."
   "Any time now."
   "Are you sure this is what they want?"
   "Yes."

Almeida came to my apartment three or four years ago. Didn't call first. Just turned up. Was passing through on her way back from the coast. Standing in the doorway with her silly hat on, a backpack. That was her travelling year, before she'd left Joe and settled down to single living. For a dreadful moment, I thought she was going to move in. With me! She came in and there was Rudolf or Adolf lying naked on the couch, on a red velvet cover. I've always liked men with soft endings to their names. She was shocked. At her age. I'm an artist, I told her. I take pictures of men. OK. And Adolf or Rudolf just lay there like a dog displaying his underside with pride.

   When she saw my family wall, all those pics I'd taken, often without them knowing I was doing it, she flipped. My God, Jessie, she said. Have you always hated us so much? And I said not always but I did hate her in that moment because she couldn't understand what I was aiming at. Like for instance a bit of truth. And the man got up off the couch and went into the kitchen to help himself to coffee. Her eyes followed him. I'd like to say hungrily but it was more that she didn't want to look at me so she looked at him.

"You just about done, Alf?"
    "Good thing your face won't show much. It keeps changing. What's on your mind?"

Alf there, wears a smock for this like some bohemian artist. There's no art about it. It's to catch the eye, that's all. Like all those Magritte images they use. I bet old Réné never figured he'd be up there on billboards. Nothing's sacred in advertising. Monet. Renoir. More déjeuners on the grass with nude variations than he ever imagined. And this is Alf's chance to show the bosses at the ad agency that he can imitate with the best of them and be original at the same time.

    We got to know each other through waiting for the elevator downstairs and talking about the disgusting choice of artwork they put up in our lobby. Only decent thing is a Remington cowboy on a bucking horse. Well this is the west. It's what people recognise in Calgary.

    Years ago I gave up on glossy magazines and cancelled my subscriptions. I'm still getting nagging letters from some of them. But they've gone the way of designer clothes and good seats at the theatre.

    It was his idea to do this in my place. He says the background wall, all those pictures, will add atmosphere.

"So what's yours, Alf?"

"What?"

"Favourite painting?"

"I haven't painted it yet."

When he's made enough at the agency, he's going to get a studio in New York and devote himself to true art. Doesn't realise that if he makes it big in advertising he won't be able to stop.

I've never asked Almeida what her favourite picture is. Maybe I'll call her when she gets home and ask. And I bet it'll be something real obvious like her life. It'll be Van Gogh. Another soft ending. She probably pronounces it *vango* which makes Dutch people wince. Which Van Gogh? I'd put my money, if there was anybody around to bet with, on the *Bridge at Arles*. She was always building bridges. Tried with me several times in our fighting days. Fool that she was, she tried to get Aunt Marge and Uncle George together one time. And that ended in tears. Lucky it wasn't blows. He's standing there in the kitchen with his arm raised and she's drawn back and I just got them in the right light.

Everybody's favourite tells something about them. A lot of people, men generally, say in a lofty sort of way, How can I pick one when there are so many? as if it would hurt them to commit. Nobody ever picks Picasso. They're afraid you'll tell them their life is falling to pieces. Dali? All that distortion? All those crutches? No way! They go for the regular, comprehensible stuff. Impressionism is going to make them seem a touch clever, what you see isn't quite what you get. So they look for the straight image or bright colour. Matisse! Everybody loves Matisse. Mention his name and they say, *Oh yes, the dancers.*

[118]

For me it's Chagall. All of it. The movement, the dream effect. And if I had to pick only one it'd be *The Young Acrobat*. Because for a short time that was me. Cliché stuff, running away and going to the circus. All that week, when the circus was in town, I went and watched them rehearse in the mornings and the clown showed me how to ride standing on the horse's back. I loved the smell, ripe manure, sawdust, sweat. If they could bottle it, they'd make a fortune. Odeur de Cirque. So when the clown left, I went too. A whole day. Before I was sent back home by the circus owner. And that picture shows the girl standing there with one leg in the air wearing a vermilion and white and green leotard and spangles and gold in her hair. And that was me for a time. OK a few days and in lots of dreams. But it was me.

To understand a painting you have to see it from the inside out.

Of course she envies my lifestyle, Almeida does. Envy is the colour of pond slime. She's off to China with him, with Joe, the quiet man. At this very moment she's in a plane flying east. And I'm here, sitting still with a house on my head, posing for a twenty-six-year-old who thinks his time is about to come. This week it's Chagall imitated, made larger. For an insurance commercial. He wants an old face, a used face, to show that the weight of a mortgage is wearing the woman down.

"I thought they used computers for this now."
"There's still room for originality."

Poor old Alf, desperate to make his mark. I can just see him going into the office next week with his pictures, his coloured boards. And the others saying, "Yes Alfredo. We'll let you know." And him never hearing another word but being put back to whatever dumb job they keep for guys like him. Making the coffee. Sucking dust out of the computers.

But not to spoil his dream of wowing them all with this brilliant idea, I'm encouraging.

"This is very unusual, Alf."
"Right."

Oh yes, I'm the one who's had all the excitement. I'm the auntie the kids used to greet with cries of joy. Truth is I'm their only auntie. I'm the one Harriet loves and tells her troubles to. Almeida's daughters. Geraldine and Harriet. You couldn't say they were spoilt exactly. But what did Almeida and Joe teach those girls about real life?

She came crying to me the first time a boyfriend let her down, Harriet did. A heart, I told her, is like your liver, it regenerates, builds itself up again. I know, I've had experience with both. So get out there, live, I said. And that was the first time she went to New Guinea. She's been travelling ever since. I like to think I got her away from leading life in a rut.

When I was living in Saudi with Ahdab, I sent photographs of the desert to Almeida to make her see that my life was the best, better than hers with Joe and the kids and all that day-after-day sameness. She'll send me a postcard from Beijing. She called to tell me they were going, I suppose in case anything happened out there, in the Orient, in the different coloured world. I wish them a good time.

[120]

I never did know what happened with Almeida and Uncle George that day. I kept out of the way. I didn't always have to run so fast and keep running, saying to myself, knowing in fact, that Dad liked me best, which he did. Like the day he said to Mom, "Jessie has the knack. She got it right in the head." And he took the picture of me with my hand on the buck's rack.

I used to hate the trips we had to take to Toronto. Mainly because I knew Dad hated them, especially he hated the way Uncle George looked at Mom and held her hand under the table. Besides in the city, there was no decent-sized wildlife. And humans are always out of season. Nearly always.

He never hunted again after that last time when he tripped over the wire trap. He apologised from then till about the week before he died when he'd stopped talking at all. I'm sorry Jess, he'd say, trying not to look at my leg. I'm sorry. And we'd have these conversations about the right way to handle a gun so that I wouldn't blame the weapon. It was an accident and no one's fault. Mom would leave us at those times and go in the kitchen and make long phone calls.

Almy tried to help but her help was like a kind of, *I've got two good legs and you're going to have a limp.* That's what it seemed to me. I guess I might have been wrong. She is basically kind and I love her; she's my sister so I have to. Photograph there of her in a navy and white dress at graduation. High School. Should've been the most exciting day of her life. For some reason she'd gone quiet. Never did know why. But did I ask?

"You must be finished."
   "Jess!"
   "What?"
   "You moved!"
   "Sorry."

I'm back in the woods with Dad. Still lying on the ferns not crying while Dad, lying where the wire had tripped him, was sobbing his head off.

"The light's wrong."
   "Does it matter, Alf?"
   "If I get this exactly right, they won't be able to resist it."
   "I've thought that myself sometimes."
   The phone's ringing.
   "Leave it," Alf says.
   "Answer it, Alf."

Too late. There's Harriet's voice on the machine. Excited. "I'll call back, Aunt Jess. Mom and Dad got off OK. See you before I go. 'Bye."
   Harriet didn't tell her parents she'd been asked to go to Rwanda. Didn't want them to worry on their vacation. She told me though. She's only going to the refugee camps. Safe, she said, as houses. If I'd had a daughter.

"Let's call it a day, Jess."
   "I should say so."

"I think I've got it."

It's my bedtime. And I have to go to work in the morning. Put on my skirt and white blouse, gold chain. Be ordinary. Shoes don't matter because I'm mostly behind the counter. *Your prints are ready Mrs. Bolsom. You took these yourself? Amazing! Twenty-four shots of your fat kids on horseback.* All this thinking's made me tired. And I'll bet I look like hell what with the weight of his toy house on my head and the colour running down my cheeks.

Alf is young and is going back to his room to work on his presentation. *Stay with me, Alf.*

He's taken the house off, and the clips that attached it to my hair and I'm dabbing at my cheeks with a tissue but what comes off on it isn't ultramarine, isn't electric blood, it has no colour at all.

The Same Destination

Harriet put her hand out and touched the face of the man beside her. He was unshaven and they were headed into danger. And they were in Africa. But they were not in a battered little steamboat and the nearest lake was a hundred miles away. Besides that her cheekbones were too well-covered to allow for any true resemblance to the great actress. Red hair but her Dad's cheerful round face which looked all right on him. Geraldine, unfairly, had drawn their mother's finer features out of the pool and of course did nothing with them, no make-up, no decent haircut. She needed to branch out, get a grip. Lose Melvin. But how could you say those things to a sister?

As kids, she and Gerry had drooled over the same movie stars but had taken different directions. There'd been no electronic device to stop them and their teenage friends watching all that romantic stuff on TV; re-runs of Bogart movies, stories of sacrifice and true love. They went starry-eyed over Omar Shãrif and James Stewart. All of it as bad for their minds as the mounds of potato chips were for their bodies. Gerry had bought into the romance. While I, thought Harriet, opted for the boat on the river.

She sucked in her cheeks and said, "Time to get up, Mr. Allnut."

Charlie stirred.

She shuddered. Couldn't believe she'd hopped into bed with a man just because he knew where he was going. Who knew where he'd been? And who with? Just because she'd gone for four months without sex. Was that it? Deprivation! Winter in Ottawa had been a dismal season for men, and men her age were mostly interested in younger, leggier women. Her trips to Toronto had been brief family times. Visiting Dad alone in the house made her depressed and probably didn't do much for him either. Staying with Mom in her apartment, listening to old family history was good for a laugh. But she often felt she was holding Mom back from appointments, classes, and all she wanted was to get back to her own real life.

And her real life meant going to bed with strangers, did it? She replied to herself sharply that her job was vital. She had to get to the camp. He knew the way. This Charlie was nothing more than a navigator. Or was he?

Before she left, back in the office in Ottawa, beige carpet, white walls, they said, We need a first-hand assessment. Check up on the local NGOs. This was a previously all right country. They said, It's dangerous, get your shots, be careful. They said, This isn't like your usual assignment. They said, Goodbye Harriet. They didn't say, We'd have sent someone else if there'd been anyone better qualified available.

Two-and-a-half weeks ago, she'd been sitting in the cafeteria at the airport in Toronto, eating tired salad and wondering why neither she nor Geraldine had offered to give their parents a decent send-off. On her own long flight, she'd figured it was because they didn't believe the two of them would actually get on the plane to China. They truly didn't want them to go. So they'd all sat there eating food they didn't want and enduring Melvin's jokes. And Mother's shirt was a cry for help made material if ever there was one.

As she'd watched Dad lead Mom off like a sheep to be sheared, she'd cried like a four-year-old left with the baby-sitter. Couldn't believe it. Some throwback memory to a time she'd felt abandoned. Had to be that. Because they would return. She would see them again.

Thinking of them, on her way to Kigali, tears had come into her eyes again for no good reason and she wasn't the crying kind, never had been. Only that on their way through the security check, they'd seemed older, smaller, even her mother had looked fragile.

Note: (first page, new notebook) *Kigali Airport. Talk to nurse on her way home to Halifax. Expect the worst. Nurse left fifteen minutes ago. Where is my meeter/greeter?*

And then he had come towards her, looked at her, at the label on her pack and said, "I believe we're heading for the same destination."

"Another organisation," he said. Though for a moment she'd wondered if he was sent to spy on her, to check because she was still, in the eyes of some in Ottawa, only a woman. His credentials showed him to be a genuine member of HRAN.

"Guy," she said and looked more closely at him. Three days she'd known him and here she was in this grubby room, sharing a bed with him. He spoke the same language but with a difference. There was something old-fashioned in him, something Boy's Own Paperish. As if he was here only for the adventure of it and might have in his pack a pair of those loose, long-legged shorts worn by Englishmen in search of places to colonise.

Photograph: *Guy in bed. Soft light brown hair falling over face. Dark hair on chest. Body of a well-nourished male aged about thirty-three-and-a-half. Eyes when open, blue and sharp. Nose non-descript. Mouth generous. Sardonic smile in dozing state.*

The car would be outside at eight-thirty, so they'd been told. She got up and put on her dangerwoman outfit: khaki slacks and shirt. Boots in case of scorpions and snakes. Hat for the sun. Notebook and kit in the backpack.

She shouted, "Ten minutes," in Guy's ear. And twenty minutes later they were in the jeep. Guy still unshaven, sat beside her peering out of the window as they started out of town towards green hills.

"It's not like a regular war," Guy said.

"I'm here to see what's going on at the refugee camp. Not to fight."

"Ha!"

The driver took no notice of them. He was a local man paid to ferry such foreigners about. He had no answer to their question about the guide who was supposed to have been with him.

Guy pulled a shaver out of his pack and began to remove a couple of days growth.

"I'd've washed but you took all the water."

"Sorry," she said.

"Very limited resources. Did they give you a gun?"

"No. But I've got a skinning knife that belonged to my granddad."

"If it comes to it, I'll throw myself in front of you."

"Sir Guy of Gisburn."

"What!"

But Harriet wasn't about to explain yet the mish-mash of her early influences, the books she'd loved best, the movies that had driven her to want a life that was unreal—romance and danger in the same moment. Those secrets could wait until she decided whether she wanted to be truly intimate with this man. Sex, considering the state of the bed and the flies, had been good. Satisfying. Fun.

Letter: *Dear Mum and Dad, I have finally met the man of my dreams. We are coming home to be married. Get Granny's veil out of the trunk.*

Guy was from Lincolnshire. His father kept sheep and wanted him to keep on keeping sheep. He was spending his life running from the flock. He'd made her laugh the night before at the image of himself being pursued worldwide by a pack of sharp-toothed ovines.

My grandfather killed animals for fun, she had told him. And they'd talked into the night about their different lives till there was nothing left to say except what kind of music they liked.

Her: Early Beatles. Classical guitar. Gorecki.

Him: Choral. Plainchant. Bon Jovi. Gorecki.

Rick, in their last session, had asked her why she felt impelled to do what she did and Harriet had made some flip answer, that it was for the men. *It's my job.* But there were other jobs for a woman with her background. There was nothing to say except that by doing what she did she might bring some light into a dark place. And that wasn't something she could say aloud to anyone.

When Geraldine had called her an idealist, it sounded like an accusation, implying wasted time and life, wasted skills. But Geraldine had no idea of the excitement in bouncing across Rwanda in a jeep with a man she'd met three days ago. Geraldine lived with Melvin. Enough said.

The road, if road it had ever been, was narrow and rocky. The jeep lurched and threw her against Guy. His shaver made a track towards his ear.

"Why are you bothering?"

"Because somewhere along here we'll come across a snot-nosed official who'll look us up and down and ask why we're here."

Why am I here? Every sense of the word. If not to understand. To make better. To cast a little light. *Always leave the campsite better than you found it.*

The nurse at Kigali had drunk her tea with a shaking hand. "Not a good time. All I can tell you is it's not a good time." And she had gone on her way, pale, altered, to tell her tale to relatives who could never understand.

They were driving through fields with small houses on them, all apparently abandoned.

Guy said, "These used to be little family farms." The driver muttered something in a kind of French she couldn't follow and Guy translated, "They shelled the camp yesterday, he says. And, by the way, his name is Marc."

There was activity ahead. People gathered at a hut beside the road. A barrier. At the barrier, a man wearing fatigues and a black beret glared at them as if they were tourists come to take souvenir pictures.

"You can't go through."

Where are you from? Again the real question. Why are you here? What's your official status? She took out her identity card from the pack and handed it to him. He looked from the picture to her and back and then at Guy.

Guy the Englishman became polite. That kind of Brit courtesy that could intimidate and also annoy because it appeared to have grown out of a deep sense of superiority.

"I'm sorry if we're in the wrong place," he said. "We were told we could get to Garoma this way."

"You're for the camp?"

"Yes."

"It's a mess. I'm not sure you should."

"We're here on behalf of our organisations. We've been authorised."

"Keep going towards that hill. You'll have to walk the last bit. It's madness sending people like you here. I can't be responsible."

They got back in the jeep. Marc turned to stare at them. If Harriet had dared, she would have taken a picture of him. His face was an image of pure disapproval.

"OK," Guy said. "We'll be fine now. Come on, Lois."

They drove on and Harriet felt the same sensation, fear, as when she and her friends had sneaked towards the house with the red door. She'd always been the one sent to tap on it and run away. Monsters lived within. Well anyway, a bad-tempered man who would come out shouting, threatening to thrash them if he caught them.

When, finally, he'd laid a complaint, it was her mother who'd been angry and told her that to invade other people's privacy was wrong. To assign demon status without reason was insulting. You have to respect people's history; her mother's creed.

Guy said softly, "Listen, Harriet, when we get back, I want you to come to the coast with me."

Water lapped on a beach. Sun shone on sand. They lay there, herself streamlined, him unshaven. They made love with a kind of passion she hadn't yet known. And had given up expecting to know. In three days could this be, and now at her age, IT? The feelings she'd learnt from those old movies were all there. A softening of old hard ideas. A simple desire to wrap herself round this man for ever.

Postcard: *Dear Mum and Dad, Have given up my job. Am going to spend my life with a guy called Guy on a beach in Zanzibar. He tastes of cinnamon.*

She sucked her cheeks in and told him she had to get back to Canada.

Ten minutes later, he said, "There used to be a mandarin grove here."

Mandarins! Harriet looked around her. Her parents would be back from China in a few days, their end-of-world trip. Costly, dangerous to their health perhaps. Her mother in that orange blouse, her Dad so anxious for them to set off. They were like two kids and wouldn't listen to any advice. Did parents ever listen to their children?

Marc spoke and Guy replied softly then turned to her and said, "You must be prepared for chaos."

The jeep stopped and the driver pointed ahead.

"Leave your stuff here," Guy said. "We might have to walk a mile or so. He'll wait."

As they walked, Guy told her he'd always known he'd meet her in Africa. A woman dressed like a man, carrying a sharp knife. A gypsy had warned him.

They walked a little farther and then in one glance, all the neat images conjured by the word 'camp' were destroyed. Bits of clothing lay scattered, tents were broken down, children and adults stared around them. It was quieter than she'd expected. But these victims could never howl loud enough to be heard in the wide world. As if they knew that, they murmured softly, expecting no response.

Guy said, "Let's find the person in charge."

Harriet's simple image of desolation fell away as she looked at the sad-eyed children and desperate adults, torn up from their roots like weeds, discarded. Lost human beings. She sat beside a woman who wanted nothing but to touch her arm and stare into her face.

What are the needs here? The question she was sent to answer. She wanted to cry. She wanted to scream and have hysterics. Find out what they need most! Those were her orders. What's the picture? How could a picture convey this dry-shit smell, the smell of misery, the sounds of utter despair.

A child in a ragged yellow garment stood nearby. Around him lay bundles, yellow, orange, grey, some tied with rope. Four goats were tethered to a tree. A red bucket lay on its side. Shadowy figures were moving slowly in the background. A woman with a water jug on her head came closer. The trees behind her were spindly. The scene carried on into the distance as if repeated by computer design. A smoky and endless field of grief. And behind the boy, just behind him, two of the bundles, two figures, a woman and child, lay sleeping. Not sleeping. Completely still.

Find out what they need! What do you need? Everything in the world. Life. Love. Secure homes. What use could a few blankets and a little money be in this place?

When Guy came back he said, "They told us to get out of here. There's trouble. If one more aid worker gets killed, they'll let no more in."

She waited to cry till they were on their way back to the jeep. Guy held her hand. For his sake or her own? It didn't matter.

"What they need!" she said and knew her voice was a screech.

Geraldine's voice in her head: You're an idealist, Harriet. You go about trying to fix the impossible. And you can't. You'll get hurt.

Aunt Jess in reply: Go for it, Harriet. Get out there and live. It's a world for heroes. Full of colour and adventure.

Like firecrackers, shots came from the direction of the camp as if the refugees were shooting their way out. Those weary, hungry people suddenly rioting.

"We have to go back," she said.

"It won't help them," he replied.

Where they'd left the jeep, there were only tyre tracks and their packs honestly set down by the road. They picked them up and began to walk.

[133]

"There's a village over there. The river. We might get a boat," Guy said, pointing east.

And Harriet, for the moment cheered, drew in her cheeks and lifted her chin and said, "Do you think so, Charlie?"

"Sir Guy of Gisburn was a villain," he said.

"Not a coward though."

"Have you always liked tough guys?"

"Is there hope?"

"There's a faint chance, when we get back, if we make enough of a fuss, a row, somebody might do something. It almost takes an army of people to let the world know. People at home have stopped listening. It's not flavour of the month any more."

"We'll shout it out," Harriet said.

Message to the world: *There is a child, standing in a field surrounded by his dead family. There are hundreds, thousands of human beings in great want, in great danger. Do something, you bastards. Get off your fat asses and help.*

The ground exploded around them. A piece of debris sliced her cheek. She put her hand to her face and felt blood. It was a long wound, from just below her left eye to her jaw. There was no pain. Strange that in such a sensitive area, it hardly hurt at all. It would leave a scar. A long scar like a duellist's badge of honour. And she was glad. In the light of what she'd just seen, a scar-free life would be quite wrong. To look in the mirror and see an unmarked face would be shameful.

Tired, she lay down beside Guy on the grass and decided that she would go to the coast with him after all. There was no time like now for holding on to some kind of love. And when she said to him, "My parents were right to go to China," she knew he understood. His smile was like an embrace that took all of her in, her past, her scarred face, and whatever the future might be.

The Emperor's Hat

The most impressive thing? They would be asked that. What was the most wonderful thing you saw? Almeida's eyes would swim at the question and she'd launch into a list full of colour and life. And Joe knew that he would sit quietly while she talked and live again the excitement of it, amazed still to think that they had been to China. For me, he would say, given the chance, it was the Emperor's hat. The one with the curtain of jewels hung from the front and the back. He put his head forward imagining that line of sparkling gems coming down in front of his face as the plane's wheels bumped down onto the tarmac and brought them back to earth.

Still dopey from the long flight, they straggled off the plane through immigration to explain themselves, half expecting the man to demand why two very ordinary people had presumed to set out on such an adventure.

Almeida looked through the glass for a familiar face in the waiting crowd. They'd told the kids not to bother to meet them, but she couldn't help hoping for even Melvin to appear before them with balloons, Harriet and Gerry to come at them with cries of relief, delighted that their parents hadn't been drowned in the Yangtse or turned to clay; a display of standing tourists.

"It's a bit of a relief they're not here," Almeida said. "We're both as tired as dogs. I'll watch for the bags."

Joe fetched a cart and loaded their cases onto it.

"We'll get a limo," he said. "A last bit of luxury." When she sat down beside him in the back she said, as he knew she would, "This reminds me of Uncle George."

They were both wide awake now, their heads full of so much that they'd seen and heard. Joe peered out the windows trying to distinguish familiar shapes in the dark, wondering all the time whether she was going to move back in with him.

"We can try it," Almeida said.

That's what Joe heard her say though he didn't recall asking, but his own voice was echoing in his head like a pea in a drum from being in the air all that time. He let the words hover, not wanting to lose them. He'd thought to tidy the place before he left and had even bought a bottle of vinegar and wiped round the floors and cupboards with it because he'd read in a household hint column that vinegar removed accumulated dirt and 'wax build-up' whatever that was.

"Do you want go to your place first for a day or two?" he asked, taking a risk but thinking to give himself time to maybe get flowers. And put food in the fridge. Get the fridge working properly. Buy a clean stove.

[137]

Right away he regretted the words because it would be easy to lose her again. She might draw back. Even after the nights in China. In Shanghai when it hadn't been too hot, they'd made love again, slowly, easily. And laughed in the old way afterwards. Laughed because they'd had to come ten thousand miles to have sex. It's going to make life expensive, he'd said to her. And she had kissed him and asked wasn't it worth it.

"What will you remember most?" she asked now.

"The crowds," he said because the emperor's hat was a small thing, a detail in a big picture.

"The man and woman in that field," she said.

"The bicycles."

"The food."

"The standing army."

"But the man and woman in the field."

Almeida too had been stunned by that pair. Their faces as wrinkled and crumpled as old paper. And yet no older than him and her. Without a word said, there'd been some connection between them. Even if it was only years lived, children born, working days.

Joe had said, "We can afford to come to their country. They'll never be able to afford to come to ours."

He'd wanted to ask the man about his work, his home, his kids. The guide waited for questions. And others in the group asked about crops and seasons and money. But there was more in the Chinese man's look than any words could tell. In that moment, he and Joe were only two men, two ordinary men. Their lives touched. They knew each other as lovers and workers and recognised each other as a pair of the world's non-talkers.

Joe's deeper thoughts rarely made it as far as his tongue. Almeida was his interpreter to the world. And perhaps it was that way with the man in the field and his wife. He sat quietly nursing the sense of loss that had returned home with him. It was, he recognised, a loss of ignorance. With loss of ignorance came the loss of a comfortable state of mind. While China had been an unknown country to him, he'd rarely considered it. And now with the image of that man and that woman and glimpses of struggle and poverty they'd chanced to see, hard working, crowded, oppressed people would hang in his mind like a row of bats in a belfry. And they would, now and then, dig their claws in to let him know they were there.

"What do you think they thought of us?" Almeida asked. "A busload of people staring at them as if they were in a zoo. Walking round their monuments."

"Rich and spoilt people," he answered.

And they were silent for a moment.

"I'll give the blue shirt to Harriet. Green is good on her. Geraldine can have the blue. Harriet! I wish she wouldn't go to those places. So easy to catch some disease. If she could settle down in Ottawa. Get herself a nice apartment. Always on the move. Where did she get that wandering from?"

"Well you, " Joe began to say.

But she kept on, "I can tell she's not happy sometimes. Wanting something. Wanting to achieve something. I know it's old-fashioned to say, and I'm the wrong one to say it, but I wish she'd find some nice man. Anyway, I'm glad they didn't come to meet us. I don't want to have to tell everything tonight. Better when we've got the pictures. We'll make a little party of it later in the week."

There was the tower just ahead of them, the lake on the right. The park on the left. A few geese were pecking about on the grass by the water. The driver would turn north soon. And Joe was holding his breath waiting to see if she would get out of the cab with him and come inside the house.

There were many things he could have said to her about the nights he had cried in the house alone. About the crazy moment when he'd begun to write an ad for the Men Seeking Women column in the weekly paper. Active man, sixties, likes—and that was as far as he ever got. He couldn't explain exactly what there was in him to attract some unknown woman. Not in chopped words for all the world to see.

"Tomorrow we'll take the film in," Almeida said.

He cherished that 'we' and dared then to ask, "Are you coming with me, Almeida?"

"Glossy or matte?" she answered.

The long flight had made her deaf. He repeated his question louder.

It was late, she said. The students would still be there and wouldn't have cleaned up. Besides wasn't their stuff packed in both suitcases? There were clothes and souvenirs to sort out. His and hers. The only thing he'd really wanted, a replica of the ancient emperor's hat was nowhere to be found. The guide had shown it to them in the museum. No less than two hundred and eighty-eight jewels she said.

Did we need to go all the way to China to have sex? In the Beijing Palace, tired feet, mind buzzing with mile-a-minute impressions, side by side. Hands touched. Lying down. Weary but not exhausted.

"Over there on the right," he told the driver and felt around for his wallet.

"I'll pay for this one," Almeida said though he'd wanted it to be his treat.

He held open the door of the cab and wondered how he would explain to her about the door missing from the dryer.

The door is missing from the dryer, she would say in that cool voice which was as good as a shriek in another woman. At school, Merry, he hadn't remembered her for years, funny how some things came back video clear. Sign of old age, they said. On the football field. Mackenzie High. *Pieces of eight, pieces of eight, pieces of nine and ten*. Cheerleaders were for the players but he was never enchanted by their jumping shouting figures. It was Merry he'd wanted. A small girl good at math with hair like gold. But one Friday Merry had shouted at him from the stands in a voice like a foghorn and his love for her died in the moment. Almeida spoke a lot but she spoke softly.

Stay here for ten minutes, he wanted to say to Almeida but waited till the taxi had driven off, leaving them and their luggage on the path. Upstairs were a couple of magazines he'd like her not to see. Not that kind of man. But lonely. Right. Not true porn. Women in black underwear. In a minute, he'd go and move them. As he opened the door to the house that had been for so long their house, he would say boldly, The door is missing from the dryer.

Then they saw the lights on inside. They stood for a moment on the path.

Almeida said, "We'll go to the box on the corner and call 911. The Ferlinis'll be in bed."

Joe said, "Burglars don't turn lights on."

A shadow moved across the window. The door opened.

"Mum. Dad."

Geraldine came and hugged them both. Her cheeks felt wet. Melvin was standing quietly behind her. For once still. For once without an instant joke. Sharon and Tyler were sitting on the couch in the living room. They stood up to greet their grandparents in a strangely formal way.

Geraldine held Almeida's hand and led her into the living room, sat her down. Joe followed. Melvin went to the kitchen. The room was full of things unsaid. Gerry had become it seemed to him taller. Not now that little girl who'd always wanted a nightlight and had seen, sometimes, monsters in the dark.

They'd come to bring flowers and food and were expecting gifts. Weren't they? Wasn't that what this was about? It had to be. Maybe they were talking, saying joyful things but his ears were deafened by the pressure of unnamed fear.

Almeida had gone totally quiet.

"You're back. You're safe," Geraldine cried.

They were standing on the Great Wall. He'd persuaded her to put the orange blouse on again. It will stand out, he'd said. And he'd taken a picture of her smiling there, happy beside one of the wonders of the world.

He was surrounded by Gerry's scent. He saw his daughter for a moment as a screaming kid clinging to

her mother's legs. Waiting for gifts. Waiting to be mol-
lified. There was a whisper in the room. Sounds never
died, they said, but lingered, dwindling. Fragments. He
caught syllables from the air and tried to put a hopeful
prophecy together.

Melvin came into the room with two mugs of coffee,
hot and sweet. Questions were unnecessary.

"There, Dad. Sit down. You must be tired."

He sat and watched the others as if they were a part
of a show he was seeing through gauze. There had to be
a welcome. It was not right they should come back to an
empty cold house and no milk in the fridge.

Gerry was glancing from one to the other of them.
They were in the house again. Both. A pair. Bookends.
Almeida would go out any minute and return with silks
draped over her arm. Gifts. The best she could afford.
He recalled the pleasure she'd taken deciding on this thing
or that.

He focussed his mind on the emperor's hat. And their
smart Chinese guide, telling how it was from the Third
Dynasty. And the emperor by lowering his head ever so
slightly could let the rows of jewels come down in front
of his eyes and block out any unpleasant sights.

He felt lips on his cheek like suction cups.

"They were looking at a refugee camp."

Melvin's voice. It echoed. Like the cave. The great
cave they had entered on cat feet. Voices in hollow spaces.
Bringing back distorted phrases. He sat up sharply. Was
she leaving? Almeida? Had they come there only to take
their mother away with them? He held his breath and
waited. He breathed out. There she was. Coming towards him. Sitting down. He sighed with relief. She was

to stay with him. She would not return to her apartment. He wanted her to stay always, not out of tiredness, not from a sense of being unable to go one step further, or only to prolong their holiday.

When the pictures came back, there she would be, standing on the Great Wall in that orange blouse. And the others on the tour seeing she was with him understood him better. He was a man who loved a woman who could boldly wear an orange blouse.

About the dryer door, she would say soon.

He bowed his head, imagining a curtain of gems in front of his face. Someone moaned. He looked up and paid attention. There was a sense of doom beating down on him. More than the noise of the plane engine persisting in his brain, a throbbing awful sound. Geraldine standing there as if dressed in black. Melvin beside her, sober. Sharon and Tyler, still. Holding their mother. *Harriet*, like a strange foreign word, hung in the air, awkwardly spoken.

Almeida knew it at once. Their news. What they had brought her. Not a welcome home message. But a tale they could hardly bear to deliver. It was written on their faces. She only needed to ask where.

"Rwanda," Melvin said and desperately Almeida wanted a map.

Where? Where? Which place. Which square of ground. Were there trees? A flower or two? So much she needed to know of the place before she could begin to ask why. As for how. She feared that answer most of all.

But she would be told. Information would come at her from all sides. There would be a hailstorm of information. But there would be no single word from Harriet herself.

"She's already home," Geraldine said. "At Bryce and Darwin. Melvin arranged it. Thursday. Give you a chance to rest."

It was an endless period of time.

There were tears. There were goodbyes. There were *see you tomorrows*.

Joe knew he was standing up. He heard the door close. Almeida swayed beside him.

"Gerry said a man's arms. Round her. Hard to separate them. Who was he? Who could he have been?"

Joe held her. And as he kept her there in his arms, he knew that there were some things in life against which the emperor's hat could be no defence at all. He felt around in his mind for decent words and all he could think of to say was, "The worst things happen when you're not looking."

Visitation

Almeida went to answer the door hoping it was a stranger come to tell her that it had all been a mistake. *That was not your daughter, Mrs. Kerwell. Your child is alive and well and will be home tomorrow.* Or maybe on the other side of the door stood a relative of the man Harriet had been with, the man who died with his arms round her. The man whose name they didn't yet know. His sister perhaps, who would speak hesitantly and later embrace her and tell her all about him.

But the woman who stood on the step was familiar and walked into the house without being asked and spoke right out.

"Hello, Almeida. Don't you recognise me? It's me. Martha. Sapph. I'd no end of trouble to find you. Couldn't remember your married name. It was Gerry in the end. Remembered her married name. That wedding."

"Come in. Well. My goodness, Martha. Come in. Sit down."

"Twelve years. I've changed."

"Dad's funeral."

"That's right. When they buried your Dad that day, I had a feeling a whole lot of deer and moose gave a sigh of relief. But. Sorry. I mean, you know. It was a sad time. And this is a sad time."

Almeida had got out of bed that morning, put on her clothes like a wind-up doll, made orange juice, remembered her mother saying that it was as easy to make a table look nice as not and got out the lace cloth and the plates with the leaf design and had sat across the table from Joe, tried to eat, tried to admire the sunny morning. And felt nothing. Now she felt surprise. And a need to be hospitable. She looked at her cousin's face, held the resemblance for a moment.

"I'll get you some coffee."

"I'd like that."

"You're looking well."

"I've come to say I'm sorry. About Harriet."

"I'll get the coffee. You just sit here."

Almeida leaned against the counter in the kitchen. The backyard looked as though an army of gophers had moved in. The beds all upturned, flowers, bulbs, scattered. For days, Joe had spent time out there digging the beds over. And over. For all the world like a gravedigger. That thought came into her head before she could stop it and the tears followed. At least he wasn't out there now. She pushed the button on the kettle and then recalled it had no water in it. All right to burn the house down but not to kill this apparently kind visitor.

[147]

Yesterday, to pass the time, she'd made a plum coffee cake and they'd both eaten a scrap of it. She'd been planning to give it to people who still had an appetite for food or put it in the freezer. Along with their feelings, hers and Joe's. Likewise frozen. Their lives were a tableau with no future beyond the day they'd returned from China laden with silk and memories. June twenty-fourth, the day of darkness.

"I'd've come to the funeral but I didn't hear till last Wednesday," Martha shouted from the other room.

"What do you take in your coffee?" Almeida called back and then, remembering her mother again, got out the cut glass milk jug and matching sugar bowl. But Martha had come into the kitchen now and was standing behind her. A scent of lemon and carnations came with her.

"I should've said, Almy. It was the shock of seeing you. I don't drink coffee. Tea. Herb tea if you've got it. And yum, some of that delicious looking cake."

In the back of the shelf was a little bag of something called *Sensualitea*. Almeida poured hot water over a couple of spoonfuls and hoped it wouldn't have any effect on Martha, at least till she got home. She had in the old days been a sexy woman.

Though this fiftyish person with her rosy cheeks, clear eyes, rounded body, had little to do with the Sapphire who'd danced in gauzy veils at the Blue Donkey. *Fine,* was the word for this woman. *Healthy* was another. *Gaudy* another still. Dark red jacket, dark red skirt, gold blouse in soft summer material, chunky gold jewellery. She brought colour to the drab house. Almeida silently thanked her for not wearing black.

They sat down with their drinks and Almeida passed her visitor a slice of coffee cake on a plate, and a fork.

"How's Joe taking it?"

What did she expect? If Martha had come to ask the usual appalling questions, Almeida would pull her up, snatch the cake away, and push her down the steps.

"You were selling real estate, Martha, last I heard."

"Briefly. The business world is not for me."

"What are you doing now?"

"Erwin and I."

"Erwin?"

"Erwin sent me really. Though I would've come anyway. Erwin and I invested together in a few acres north of Aurora. We guide people to healthy attitudes. Not happiness, Almeida. Nothing unrealistic like that. Erwin always says that if God had meant us to be happy, he'd've given us four legs and a tail and the ability to leave large pats of shit in fields for people to step in."

Almeida wondered why, in her deep distress, this vision had been sent to her. She looked at Martha and yes, she was real, she was there, she was eating a mouthful of coffee cake and the crumbs were spilling onto her lap and from there to the floor.

"How do you make this?"

"The usual way. As long as the plums are firm there's no problem with it."

"Mmm. You could give me the recipe."

Almeida waited. Dark times allowed for this. Every now and then a clown appeared on the stage to distract, annoy, leave you feeling worse off. This time a clown with a painted face and a big red smile.

"So what we do, me and Erwin, we take in the disturbed, people in sorrow, and we offer them alternatives, another way of seeing what they see."

Almeida helped herself to a good-sized piece of cake. No way she could get through this conversation without nourishment.

"We'd make room for you and Joe. A week at our place, only six hundred dollars. A reduction for relatives. I could tell you stories of our successes."

The bite of cake stuck in Almeida's oesophagus. It would never go down, she knew it. Like a stone it lay there and would be there when they buried her.

Martha's eye lighted on the photograph of Harriet in her hiking outfit.

"She was brave, eh. To go and do what she did. And all that among strangers."

To stop her, Almeida nearly shouted, "We were sorry to hear about your Dad."

"Dad. Oh yes. Well it's ages ago. He'd've been ninety-seven next month. He used to ask after you Almeida. Always a soft spot."

Wrong diversion. Almeida didn't want right now to think about Uncle George. But Martha continued.

"When your Dad married your Mom, it hurt him so much. He told me all about it."

"Told you?"

"I am his daughter, Almy. And you were kind of like her, like your mother. It drove him crazy. Love is the weirdest thing. By the time he married my Mom, he'd mainly gotten over it. Marge never forgave him for leaving, did she? I guess that was obvious. All those years of her life. The whole thing had a kind of warping effect on him. That and the war."

There were tortures of various degrees. Being led through her own past by a relation who saw it all differently and some parts of it up close was a cruelty on this day. Why not the rack, oh Lord! Why not a plague of frogs!

"How's Sue?"

"Sue has her life. I have mine."

Thoughts of her sister stopped Martha in her flow but not for long.

"She's taken on this martyr role. The only one who does anything for Mom! I just do what I do more quietly that's all. Did you and Jess have this problem? Well I guess your parents passed on—I mean before it came to arguing about who looked after them."

At least, and Almeida couldn't stop the thought coming into her mind, my daughters now won't be arguing about that. To hold back her tears she found another question.

"Tell me more about your—what is it? Retreat?"

"First and foremost is nourishment. That's my department. Nothing like sitting down to a nice meal, well set out, to take people out of their trouble. We run our sessions from Monday to Friday and the Monday dinner is always the same. Blue cheese soufflé, appetiser. Fish, the best we can get that day, main course. Salmon, sole, cod provençale. And then Pear Hélène. You can't serve mousse if you've started with soufflé. Or it might be chocolate praline pie. It's not really a pie. Pear Hélène is the favourite. And on Mondays, the wine is free."

Almeida wanted to cry out, What has this to do with my daughter? My loved child? But she sat and let the images of food dangle there between them.

"We're careful about coffee. Stimulants can add to grief. And basically we're out to soothe."

"After nourishment?"

"On Tuesdays we serve red meat. We like people to approach their anger."

Almeida saw herself stalking her anger as a beast through the jungle, hissing and growling, setting traps for it, having it turn on her when, finally, she came face to face with it.

"We offer a course on grief control."

A dam. A dyke. Great turbines turning grief into electricity, fuelling a city, a use for it at last. And out there some Doctor Strangelove inducing grief in people because the industrial world needed cheap energy. Her and Joe grieving for the sake of streetlights, or perhaps, for a rock band. Keeping the guitars and the synthesiser going at full blast.

"Do you get a lot of clients? Customers?"

"We're full till September."

"People know in advance that they're going to be in mourning? In trouble?"

"We make space for immediate problems. We are elastic. What I could do for you and Joe."

"I don't think we're quite ready."

"Almeida. I don't want you to think I just came to drum up business."

"No Martha, no."

And for a moment, Almeida saw a look of Uncle George, a kindness and sympathy in the face opposite, but it disappeared quickly, and there was the crafty look of the old Sapphire who knew her audience and responded to it by taking off another veil.

"Is Joe in?"

"He had—has some business to attend to." He was with Geraldine at the bank sorting out Harriet's affairs. She'd offered to go too but he'd shaken his head and gone out without a word.

"Did Jess come to the funeral?"

Now she wanted a list of the mourners!

"Jess has a bad back. She fell, slipped on something in her apartment."

"I see."

"She and Harriet were close. She would have come if she could. She's in a lot of pain."

"I guess I shouldn't be too long. But now we're in touch. Erwin says family is very important. Nothing takes its place."

"How did you meet Erwin?" Almeida asked, having in mind a long-haired evangelical swindler.

"I was standing on the street corner not knowing which way to turn and there he was. It was the eyes you know. He has these piercing eyes that look deep into you. I haven't reached the depth of him yet. I may never but I'm enjoying the looking. He's a lot younger than I am but we don't find that a problem. People take me for his mother. He's very good about the place. The heavy work."

She was still Sapphire. The tales of Uncle George's life with his second wife and their two daughters might well have been true. But maybe it was Uncle George's own nature that created his difficulties. The women in his life had not had an easy time of it either.

Martha leaned forward and said, "Family is family, Almy, and whatever we've done or not done in the past

[153]

I want you to know that my sympathy is with you. The loss of a child."

Almeida's only desire was to end the visit before the scream she was holding back rose to the surface. She stood up and moved towards the door.

"It was good of you to come," she said.

"Now I've found you."

"We'll be going away soon."

"I'll leave these brochures with you. Think about it. It might be just what you need."

"Goodbye, Martha. Give my regards to Erwin."

Anger. That was what Almeida knew she was feeling as she closed the door. All these people figuring what they needed right now, she and Joe. Casseroles, company, cards, flowers, calls. And that woman had come here in her bright clothes, had deliberately sought them out in their distress. Made an effort. Looked for them. So that she too could oppress, take away with her a little of their own sorrow and share it. With somebody called Erwin for Chrissake! And all she and Joe wanted was time with Harriet, the one thing they couldn't have.

She sat down and all the tears she'd been holding back since the day of the funeral poured out of her. She grabbed a cloth and held it to her face. She felt herself shaking and didn't try to stop. Empty, exhausted, the cloth soaked, her hands damp, she heard the door open. She ran upstairs and washed her face, changed her sweater and went down to face the rest of the day.

She said to Joe, "You just missed my cousin Martha."

"They all come, don't they," he replied.

"I'll go get something for dinner," she said. "And we'll go for a walk tomorrow. Next week, we'll have Gerry and the family round."

He looked up and gave her his best attempt at a smile. "I'll fix the swing."

She began to say that Sharon and Tyler were grown and their legs would touch the ground but instead she said, "They'll like that."

Joe said, "It will get light again. One of these days."

She knew he was right.

She reached for her recipe book and found the page she wanted. Danish blue, butter, milk, eggs. More fat than she and Joe were supposed to eat. But with a salad. Brown bread. The soufflé dish with the green fluted edge. She set the book down sharply. For several minutes sorrow had released its grip on her. How could she do that? Withdraw all that grief from Harriet? A calmer voice said, Harriet doesn't know. Harriet is not aware.

"I won't be long, Joe," she said.

She stepped outside into the heat. The air smelt of sulphur. There was traffic, there were people, there were young women. She wanted to go back into the house and close the door and hide from anyone who might come up to her and say the terrible words she'd heard so often lately: *Life must go on.* But she went out and walked along the street to the store because nothing was more important right then than to buy four ounces of blue cheese.

Heart

Almeida woke up in the night and cried out. She sat up and opened her eyes. In her dream someone had been trying to kill her by pressing her face down into the floor. Her heart was pounding with fear. She looked over at Joe in the other bed, sleeping callously through her peril. She put her bedside light on, thankful that she didn't, as her grandmother would have done, have to light a candle and then contend with shadows on the wall.

It was nearly four o'clock. Joe was snoring lightly, a gentle, purring sound. Her heart was taking its time to slow down to normal. Thumping at her chest wall. She'd seen them at the meat counter, hearts, but had never chosen to cook one. Fried heart. Grilled heart. Braised heart. It all sounded too much like eating a soul. Her own heart she knew looked nothing like those on a butcher's block. It wasn't a smooth moist thing. It had lately been torn and cut into strips. But it kept on beating. And over time the strips would grow together, leaving scars. It was a gnarled and knotted thing, her heart.

Heart, the cookery books said, is firm and rather dry and is best prepared by slow cooking. It may be stuffed.

Suppose, she thought, I've only got ten good years left, ten weeks, ten days, ten hours. Her life ahead narrowed to a point, no more than a cart track with a stop sign at the end of it. Or maybe this tough heart would go on beating for another thirty-odd years and there she would be trying toothlessly to blow out a hundred candles. She'd walk into traffic rather than that, not caring whose day she ruined or who had to go home and say, I killed an old lady this morning.

Her heart had slowed down but her mind had woken up. She got out of bed and went downstairs. September. Still dark. The days were getting shorter. She could hear raccoons doing whatever they did at that time. She made herself a cup of tea and sat down on the couch to listen to the sound of a day starting up. Wheels on the road. Early or late people going by. The thud of Heavy Metal coming closer then moving off; a car with its windows open. A couple of streets away a dog began to bark and she was pushing a stroller on a path through grass and the child's hand was reaching out to pick flowers along the way. The child's face was hidden by a baseball cap pulled down over its eyes. The child offered the flowers to her, cornflowers, daisies, dandelions and when she reached out for them, the child disappeared leaving the bouquet in her hand and a bell ringing in her ears.

Joe was already dressed. He went to the door while

she ran upstairs out of sight. It was nine o'clock. The man from Ottawa had made his way into the house as though he had a right to be there. She could hear the low rumble of their voices. Both of them waiting for her, worried that she might be about to withdraw her consent. Might scream at him and tell him to leave them alone. No wonder her sleep had been disturbed, it was the day of exposure.

Jean had given her advice about what to wear but had refused to come and share in the experience. It's family time, she said. Don't wear anything dark. A nice collar. Not much jewellery. Almeida had put on weight since that June day. After cousin Martha's visit, her cookery books had become a source of comfort. Surprising since her appetite had gone and all food tasted alike. Of nothing. Her black skirt was tight at the waist but she put it on anyway, would hold herself in. The white shirt at least was loose. She put the gold chain round her neck. Touched her lips with Golden Glow. Gathered her nerve ends together and went downstairs.

When she entered the room, the man from Ottawa was looking at a picture of Harriet aged sixteen, her cap pulled forward. The unmade girl on the threshold of an unplanned life.

The man from Ottawa stood up to greet her and said, "Mrs. Kerwell," as though she might have forgotten her own name.

The man from Ottawa had put his briefcase down beside him. His suit had an expensive sheen to it. Dark blue with a hint of a grey stripe. Discreet.

"We need your signature, "he said. "And your advice, your input."

[158]

She looked at Joe who had been listening to this Capital-Speak for the twenty minutes it had taken her to wash and dress and wake up and lose the dream of the child.

"Ms. Kerwell was a brave and devoted member of the team. Her visit to the camp and her . . . death, along with Guy Brooke-Davis, has shed a light, if you will, on the worst of the refugee camps. Something is being done. The wheels are in motion."

Almeida felt a moment's pity for the man. He had come to tell her that her daughter hadn't died in vain. And while he was speaking he knew, he must know, that what he was saying was a travesty, a hateful laundering of facts. Like officers in previous wars who'd had to tell parents that their children had given their lives variously to save democracy, the free world, to make the world safe for capitalism, or simply to beat down some upstart nation, he was there to offer her and Joe an unwanted consolation prize.

"I'll be back in a minute," she said.

In the kitchen, she put the kettle on, got out the filter, the coffee, tray, cups, milk; mechanical actions. No one took sugar now, surely. Why wasn't this fellow out there doing something useful, looking after the interests of sugar-growers in the Dominican Republic for instance. But the van was at the door already and when she looked out of the window there was a girl putting traffic cones up the street and a sign that said, Sound recording please drive slowly.

Last week when she d told Joe about the man's call, Mr. Di Franco, from JCTV, Joe had slammed his fist down on the table. A new belligerence had come on him since Harriet's death. He was a father who hadn't protected his daughter from danger. No one was going to harm her now. Yet there he was sitting in the other room, meekly listening to words she could faintly hear.

Mr. Di Franco was saying, "You know how much we valued your daughter's reports. She was a fine observer of conditions. A clear-sighted and devoted worker."

There was no accounting for men, what they would put up with. Now he was telling Joe that the video would help set up a fund in Harriet's name.

She set the tray down on the coffee table and said, "You're going to use her for charity?"

"She loved her work."

To stop him from telling them that Harriet would have wanted to die like this, from getting any more into the swampy area of ends and means, she said, "Are you thinking of using her photograph?"

"We'll have to black the room out," he replied. "The unit will try not to create any mess."

"How long?"

"Fifteen minutes of actual air time followed by footage from the camps."

Begin with the elderly grieving parents, flashing to happier times, to the school pictures of Harriet winning ribbons for running faster than anyone in her age group. Why had she failed to run when it was most important! Back to the interior of her parents modest home. A perfect background for a sob story.

"I meant how long will it take to make?"

"When you wring people's hearts, you wring their purses too."

Had he really said that or was she still dreaming? No

[160]

one could have been so crass. She gave him the benefit of the doubt and offered him coffee. He shook his head. He was probably used to a superior brew.

"Anything we can do to alleviate distress."

She stared him into answering her question.

"Probably most of the morning, Mrs. Kerwell. As I explained, they'll try not to disturb you too much. But it's important to get a kind of naturalness to this."

If it was natural, I'd be screaming. I am holding my self together for Joe's sake. For Harriet.

"If you could just sign."

As she wrote her name, Almeida felt as if, any moment, he would hand her a bag containing thirty pieces of silver.

The man from Ottawa had gone but his space in the room was still occupied. Joe was sitting beside the tray with its empty coffee cups, two used, one clean. As if his head were clear glass, she could read his thoughts: *What would Harriet have wanted?*

She took the tray and went to the kitchen. She knew that Harriet would have laughed and said, *Let them do what they like. What does it matter now?*

Joe had followed her. He was standing by the window looking out at the holes he had dug in the back yard.

"Whose distress?" he asked.

Sharon and Tyler arrived, excited but knowing enough to be subdued. Sharon had loved Harriet too, wanted to be like her. Had cried her share of tears. Geraldine and Melvin followed. Melvin was a quieter man lately as if he mourned Harriet as much as all of them. Almeida forgave him a good deal for that.

She poured lemonade for them all. Got out the cookies. It was a day when sustenance was required.

Jess came in walking with two canes.

"See, I've made progress," she said.

Almeida kissed her sister and gritted her teeth. Jess would as usual take up more than her share of the space, talk to the TV crew in their own language while she and Joe withdrew to the background. *This is my sister, the one who wears a house on her head.*

"Hi, Aunt Jess," Sharon said. "I saw your ad. Neat."

"It made a young man very happy," Jess replied and made them all laugh.

False light filled the room. The woman with the loud voice said, "Let's just make sure your nose isn't shiny." And then the cameraman took over. Gave them orders. Over here. There. That's right. Now if you could just. Mr. Kerwell. Beside the photograph. Kids to one side, please. The sister here. Now then. A few words. You know about her as a child. Something that showed how she might grow up. Adventurous.

Joe was saying, "She always cared about other people," as if someone had written a script for him.

Geraldine began to tell them about the games they'd played as children but couldn't stop herself from crying.

Jess said to the cameraman during a break, "Tell me what your favourite painting is."

Almeida said for the fourth time, "How long will this take?"

And then it was two o'clock. Melvin had taken the children home an hour before. Geraldine had gone upstairs to lie down, said she'd follow later. The cables were rolled. The producer told them it would be great, a little editing was all. Beautiful. Sorry. Very sorry. You'll see the tape first. Only right. It would be good, he could feel it. He always knew. The woman and the other man, Bob, nodded. Yes, he was a wizard at knowing.

"See you," they said. And were gone.

Almeida felt tired to her bones. Joe was sitting in his chair like a statue. Then Jess called him to come into the kitchen.

"I need help, Joe."

Forty years ago, thirty, face it, twenty, Almeida would have felt jealousy rise up in her at the thought of them together in another room. Even now she wondered what the hell they were doing. But moments later, Jess limped into the room followed by Joe carrying a bottle of champagne and three glasses.

"I put it in the fridge this morning," she said. "I thought we might need it."

"To celebrate?"

"Yes, Almeida." Jess opened the bottle carefully and poured letting the bubbly liquid spill over the outside of the glasses.

"Don't say it," Almeida cried out to her sister, hating her as she had never done. "Don't tell me she died doing what she wanted. Don't tell me she didn't have to grow old and get Alzheimer's and lose her teeth and start falling down in the street. Don't tell me she didn't suffer. And that she had excitement and had travelled. I can't bear it. This isn't fair. It isn't right. I won't listen. What about the music she won't hear, the books she'll never read. And the children. And the last years of our lives. And the words I want to say to her. And the times we might have had. She never saw the gown I bought her in Beijing. It has dragons on it. Green silk."

Geraldine was in the doorway asking, "What's the shouting?"

Jess said, "Get yourself a glass, honey." Then she moved to her sister's chair and put her hand on her shoulder and said, "I'm saying she knew what love was. That's all, Almeida."

Almeida swallowed her tears and her heart stopped thudding.

"She knew what love was," Jess repeated.

Joe looked up like a rabbit peering out of a deep hole into unexpected light.

"I guess that's kind of a good thing to know," he said.

He took his glass and raised it and after a long moment, Almeida did the same and smiled at Jess: To Harriet. To Harriet's life. To Harriet's knowledge of love.

"What's your favourite painting?" Jess asked as if they were ten again, playing a game.

Almeida thought before she replied. "It used to be *The Bridge at Arles* but now I think it's that other bridge, the Japanese one where people are carrying heavy weights and it seems to be raining."

"Why are we drinking champagne?" Geraldine wanted to know when she came back into the room.

"Because," Almeida said, "it's good for the heart."

Heroine

"You were mad because she married the fat Greek."

"I'm only saying she wasn't a heroine."

It was their regular November argument but Almeida's heart wasn't in it. Her mind, what shreds of it she could gather together, was drifting about like a hawk in a thermal current. She failed to make her usual remark about the blood so Jean couldn't go on about the pink suit, and there was silence between them. Meanwhile the psychiatrist in her mind was saying, *stress, stress, stress.*

She'd got up that morning, asked Joe how he'd slept, gone downstairs to the kitchen and made enough toast for two. Listened for him moving about. She'd set out two mugs on the counter and then caught sight of the birdhouse in the backyard. She put one of the mugs back in the cupboard and chopped up one slice of toast for the sparrows. The birdhouse still startled her. The way

[165]

he'd made it out of three sections of her head so as not to waste the wood. The front was made of an old piece of maple. Thank heaven he hadn't thought to use her mouth as the door. *It was anger, Joe, wasn't it. You were angry that we'd grown older, that you'd retired. You had no office to go to. That I have grey hair and lines and let's not think about my body. You were taking it out on wooden blocks. You couldn't stop.*

"You all right, Mrs K?" The Voice yelled over the fence.

"I'm fine."

The Voice had moved in next door after Jean's defection to the outer edges of town.

Almeida hurried inside. She didn't want to have to explain herself to a stranger. She was cold. She must've been standing out there in her slippers and housecoat with the empty plate in her hand for fifteen minutes. Must've looked like some idiot statue.

She managed to get her wits together to make it downtown. Habit had drawn her footsteps to the restaurant, to the table in the window. She hadn't dared drive the car with her mind in this state. She didn't want to be reduced into a humorous item in the paper: *Elderly woman drives into bakery window. Buns crushed.*

She focussed her senses on the immediate. Jean opposite her was wearing an unusual blue sweater with green stars appliquèd onto it. A necklace of ceramic fish hung round her neck. She'd touched her cheeks with dark rouge. The familiar face looked sharper than usual as if Jean had become, overnight, a bright intellect, a shining media star. She'd touched up her eyelashes with mascara.

On Almeida's plate lay a warm bread roll. In front of her a was plate of salad she couldn't remember ordering and on Jean's place mat, a bowl of soup.

"Is that chowder?" she ventured to ask.

"You know it is," Jean answered. "Almeida?"

But Almeida's brain had split into shards. Paths were crossing. Sound effects were dazzling. Music interfered. Conversations buzzed in her head. After breakfast she'd tried to count backwards in sevens and got stuck at sixty-four. *This is not Alzheimer's.* I was in love once. I have been in love. People die. It happens. It would happen. A day would come when the world woke up and Joe wasn't there. When she wasn't there. *Panic, panic, panic. Think calm.*

"Last night I was dreaming about an island, palm trees, blue sea. I was a mermaid."

"That's an escape dream," the new sharp Jean said.

Escape! That woman in her pink suit, young, younger than Harriet when she was called on to be a hero, had been trying to escape from the scraps of her husband's brain. What would Harriet have done in her place? Harriet would never have allowed herself to be sold for political advantage. And she'd never worn pink after she was old enough to buy her own clothes.

"Perhaps you need a trip. You were dreaming of Florida. A vacation would do you good. There's nothing you can do for Joe. He's comfortable. Looked after."

"They say that if you talk, they can hear. So I tell him what's happened. The trouble is not much happens. My day is pretty much a got-up-had-breakfast-cleaned-house kind of routine. Why are you all dressed up?"

"I told you Dwayne showed me how to access the net. You get into this site and there are men. Men who want to meet women."

"Women our age?"

"There are always older men, Almeida."

"I've seen them. And anyway, it's dangerous."

"It's quite safe. You meet them in a public place. And you talk."

"So how old is he?"

"He's only a little younger."

"Ah."

Guy ropes were being cut. With a sharp knife. Joe and now Jean were abandoning her, leaving her to float free which once she might have loved to do. Now, more than anything, she wanted ties.

"Don't look like that, Almeida. I'm not prepared to feel that my life is over. What happened to Joe has made me aware of how short life is. I've met Bill twice now. He's kind, very gentle."

"Where does this Bill live?"

"That's what I want to tell you. Why we're having lunch today instead of tomorrow."

"Where!"

"Huntsville. He's taking me to see his condo next week."

Almeida turned away. She was trying to gather her senses together so that she could say something generous. Something like, well that's wonderful old friend. But all she could think of were three names, Harriet, Joe, (he could go on like this for years, Mrs Kerwell), and Jean. She became a dull balloon drifting over the lake.

"That'll be nice."

"I read a piece in the paper that said she was angry."

"If you'd read something besides all that fantasy stuff."

"Bill likes it too. He has all those games."

Games!

"I'll stick to biographies."

"Then you're missing out on something. That's all I can say. Missing out on a lot."

"The world is not about to be taken over by aliens."

"You see you have no idea."

Joe was lying back on the bed. His left hand, the one that still functioned, was smoothing the sheet like an iron.

Brent said kindly, "We've been for our walk. I think he moved a toe today, Mrs Kerwell."

It was a fiction they both conspired in. He smiled at her and talked to her for a moment as if Joe was his sole care and a dear one at that. But then he was off to another bed, another helpless man.

What was Joe to Brent but a low-maintenance patient who had enough visitors to relieve the nurses of some watching, enough to show that he was cared for?

"Hello Joe. Time for our afternoon chat. You won't believe this but Jean has got herself a boyfriend. From the computer. The web. The spider's web. What do you think of that? What can she want with a man at her age? I ask you. It can't be sex. I mean how often did we make love lately?"

She lowered her voice. The flap-eared woman who sat beside Ernie in the next bed was leaning closer. Ernie could still talk, make sounds at least, but his sister didn't have much to say to him.

"I know what you're thinking, Joe. You're telling me

I wasn't there for what could've been two years of prime time sex. Maybe not prime time but good. Well you were preoccupied. You had other things on your mind. You were carving those heads for me, were you? Well all I can say is, it didn't look like it. You have to understand. So OK I didn't give you time to explain. I was fed up, Joe. I got tired of waiting for you to turn round and notice I was there in the flesh, dammit.

"China was good though, wasn't it? You were like your old self. You made me feel I was still—I hate that word 'still'—attractive. She's old but she can 'still' do this, that or the other. We might, over time, have become real lovers again. But then—Harriet. That was it for you. Game over.

"I'm feeling very scattered, Joe. My mind seems to have fallen to bits. If I talk to anyone about it, they're going to say, no wonder, Almeida, what with Joe ill you with the house and everything to look after. I should have asked you about the water heater.

"They tell me you can hear so I keep on. I hope I'm not boring you. You are looking a little bit better today. More colour.

"I've been reading a book about Tibet. There's a new movie out. It's a sad book. They were better off when they were remote and mysterious. We didn't see the bad side of China, did we. Not allowed. I'll read a bit of it to you tomorrow. You get up off that bed and we'll go to the movie together.

"I haven't cleaned your workbench up. I told you that yesterday. You have the garden seat to finish.

"If Jean hooks herself up with this man, he's called Bill—so he says—she'll move to Huntsville. He's told her he has a condo there. It might as well be Vancouver. I never told you about the man I met on the sea wall there. Perhaps I won't just now.

"Gerry's probably told you all their news. Sharon got in at Western. Little Sharon. Our first grandchild.

"And one other thing. Helen, remember Helen from when I worked at the surgery, wants me to call this friend of a friend. He's looking for a companion for his mother. A dog might do as well, you'd think. A job. What do you think? Something to take me out of myself. Stop me fretting about Jean. I'm more worried about her than myself. She could be making a terrible mistake. How does she know this man isn't after her bit of money or isn't an axe murderer?

"I saw your eye move then, I did. Nurse! His eye moved."

It has to do with the light.

"Do you hear music, Joe? Do memories play through your mind? When we danced. When we danced and never wanted to stop. I think I have to go now. I'll come back tomorrow.

"Should I call this man or not? I'll go and maybe find out what he wants, Helen's bridge partner's friend."

"Uncle George used to walk in the parade."

"I didn't know I was still wearing it," Jean unpinned the red poppy and put it in her purse.

"Those old guys."

"Can you imagine what it was like. Going off to die. Knowing the odds were you wouldn't would come back."

Almeida saw Uncle George as a young soldier, marching in that endless khaki stream winding its way up a ship's gangplank.

Jean was eating a ham and cheese sandwich. Bill had told her she was too thin.

"And now they're selling her stuff off."

"It comes down to that for the famous. And the rich. Remember that awful scene in *A Christmas Carol* where Scrooge can hear them stealing his bedding. Now it's the chair she sat in. The rings she wore. They won't be selling your stuff at auction or mine."

Almeida looked out of the restaurant window. Most of the leaves were down. A woman was pulling her hood up as if winter was following her down the street. Fear. That was it. The fear that out of the sky or up from the ground would come the blow that would put her below it forever. Relatives would gather. The children would cry but Joe, if he survived her, would hardly know. The empty space would soon be filled.

"When I was a kid, we had a picture of The Lady of Shalot. It hung in the kitchen near the stove. It was spattered with grease. I used to think that was what it took, being a heroine. Drifting on in a boat, hair down to your waist. Alone. My Mum used to read Tennyson aloud. *She loosed the chain and down she lay.* Almeida! You looked like you'd gone to sleep."

"What were you saying?"

"I think it didn't matter what her actions were."

"You're saying she was a heroine anyway?"

"I'm saying we all are. In different ways."

"So what's it about?"

"It comes down to being kind to one another."

"Sometimes you have to act."

They paid the bill and went out on to the street. Jean turned right to meet her man at Grain and Berrit. Almeida turned left and stared in the empty window of a store for rent until Jean had gone round the corner. She kept to the wall, moved slowly, well out of sight. If the man was desperate-looking, she would go in and drag her friend away. Kicking and screaming if need be.

Jean, the new perky image of Jean, was sitting at a table near the counter looking at a man who was looking back at her with what could only be called fondness. *I'll throw up. I'll throw up.*

What was Jean saying in there? *I'd like to move to Huntsville but my best friend needs me right now. She has always* . . . . Or was it, *I've been waiting for you all my life, Bill. It's never too late for love.*

Fuck it! Almeida was surprised. She hated that phrase. But it was the only one that fit the moment. Fuck it! I have to get out of this. I've become someone who looks in at life. A watcher. The kid outside the candy store. There is still life out there. There is! She moved too quickly and had to wait for the pain in her thigh to settle down.

When she got home, she looked round the house. Before too long, she would have to get a smaller place. It was time to discard, to unload.

She packed up Joe's clean pyjamas and the new toothbrush ready to take to him next day and sat down to dial the friend of a friend of Helen's phone number. She listened to the rings and went on talking with Jean in her head.

[173]

An ordinary person would never have got over it. Would have had nightmares, been locked away.

So marrying a Greek ship owner was the next best thing?

Rich people have different options.

If you strip them down, their feelings have to be the same. As yours and mine.

Go ahead and do what you have to do, Jean. And good luck!

Tapestry

The lion motif was continued in the lampshades. Smaller, gentler lions served as bookends. They were there again in coloured thread in the cushions. Nothing in the room was new except the computer. The desk itself with its slim legs and scroll top was a period piece. There'd been one like it on the Antiques Roadshow last week, valued at twenty thousand dollars. Almeida looked at the man behind it, delicate features, balding on top, little moustache. Mr. Speight was tapping at his keyboard and paying no attention to her. She wondered if his password to the outer world was *lion*. She tried to make out lion heads in the pattern of the Persian rug. It was worn here and there; a path trodden by slight feet in boots, in tapestry slippers. But the design in the rug had been woven long ago by foreign hands.

"Are you," she asked, "a hunter?"

She'd nearly turned back from the stone lions at the door, but Geraldine's birthday was not far off and she wanted money to buy her a gift. Something grand to make up for all those years being married to Melvin. "You don't understand him, Mom," Gerry said. *Oh yes I do, honey.*

Besides that, everyone had been telling her to get out of the house, do something. She would become ill herself if visits to the hospital were her only occupation. Helen had given her the phone number and in her bossy way said, "Now you make sure you call, Almeida."

So here she was, out of the house, looking at Helen's friend's friend, dumbly waiting for this stranger to pay attention to her, wanting to ask why he didn't go to an agency and hire a qualified care-giver.

Mr. Speight, responding to some call she couldn't hear, got up suddenly to leave. From the doorway he said, "I won't be a moment." And then, "We inherited the lions."

It was a part of the city which had a different history from the areas she knew. People were bequeathed more than money, they were left things which weighed heavily on them all their lives. *With these oil paintings you inherit a great responsibility, my child. With these lions, I thee wed.*

Early in the century which would very soon be 'last century', other Speights had moved about in this room planning for their immortality. Women in graceful skirts who never forgot their class had lingered here. A scent of stale dried rose petals hung about the place.

A foreign woman of twenty-five or so, a woman with a similar name to her own, is feeling the cold, standing

[176]

nonetheless by the window, looking out at the first early snowfall. She draws her shawl around her.

"Adélie is afraid of sitting too close to the fire," the figure in the corner remarks.

Adélie moves to a chair by the fireplace and says in a sulky voice, "I was watching the snow."

"Allow me," a gentleman murmurs and moves the embroidered screen nearer to protect her delicate skin from the heat.

And Adélie says, "Tomorrow I shall go back to Belgium."

"No my dear, we can't allow that," the aunt states from her corner.

Another gentleman moves his neck in his stiff collar like a turtle, lifts the tails of his coat and warms his seat at the fire.

"I thought the pheasant rather over-cooked," he says.

The other man slyly moves closer to Adélie and takes hold of her hand. Will she slap his face, draw back, act as if she hadn't noticed? She lets her hand lie in his, limp as a fish.

Her aunt, ten feet tall in the long velvet gown, not seeing, says, "We'll arrange the wedding. Your poor mother wanted you to be married in this garden."

Adélie hears 'buried in this garden' and looks up startled. Though to her, the meaning is the same either way.

Almeida sat on. A woman in the role of servant came in and set a tray down beside her, a cup of coffee and four cookies on a blue and white china plate. Mr. Speight, she said, wouldn't keep her long. Other housekeepers had moved around here too. With the same kind and nurturing look, they had brought drinks to their employers and comfort to the house. *Dedicated, devoted*, were the words uttered at their deaths or when they were handed that final cheque which would in no way serve as a decent pension.

"I'm fine," Almeida replied. "Thank you."

What would Joe think to see her sitting in this room waiting to be offered, or not, a granny-sitting job. But Joe had given up thinking. He had opted out. She pushed the tears back and considered the situation.

Two weeks at most. Older woman preferred. Sherlock Holmes stories began like this, with a few lines in the situations vacant column. An unsuspecting person goes to a door and is invited in. To wait. Till the woman in tapestry slippers comes forward.

Adélie says again, "I can see no point in staying here."

"Money?" asks her aunt.

"I will earn it." Adélie is proud.

"Our family has never stooped to paid labour."

"I am only a distant relation."

The aunt returns to the piano and sits down and begins to play a nocturne which could be a waltz.

Harry is asking Adélie to dance. He places his gloved hand on Adélie's back. She glides across the carpet in his embrace and he whispers, "Come away with me." She says, "This music wasn't made for dancing."

Frederick is the one who holds the keys to the family fortune. Adélie must marry him in order to survive. But she loves the rogue Harry who has a slight moustache and will soon be bald.

"Adélie has danced in Paris," Harry says.

"We shall not mention that," the aunt puts in.

Harry is just back from his latest hunting expedition in Africa. He was in Bloemfontein with the fifth division. At Spion Kop, fighting the Boers, he discovered how much he loved the country. The spears on the wall in the hall, the shield made of leopard skin, are his. When the war was over and he no longer had licence to kill men, he returned to Africa to kill the animals.

Harry says, "Your king has interests there."

Adélie whispers, "I cannot go with you."

Harry says, "My next lion will be for you."

Adélie replies, "Oh Harry, if only it could be so."

"We'll hunt together."

For a moment she is gliding through the undergrowth with him, lying down under a canopy of stars.

"You were meant for me, little Belgian cousin."

"Cousin at third remove."

"I would feel the same if you were my sister," Harry says. But then perhaps does not say that. Passion shines in his eyes, his fingertips play a scale on her back. The others are watching. Adélie returns to her place.

The housekeeper came back and invited Almeida to follow her. Down a long hallway. This was when the body would be found in the library, and in no time a detective would be asking why she had come to the house in the first place. What did she have to do with this family? They would rummage through the newspapers and find no advertisement. Helen would deny having given her the phone number. Gerry would lie for her and say she had been with her all day. The court case would eat up her savings and she would die on the street. *I am innocent*, she cried.

The old lady was sitting upright in her chair and Mr. Speight was beside her. He stood when Almeida entered.

"Mother, this is Mrs. Kerwell."

"Good afternoon," Almeida said.

It was a room of distinction. On a low table sat a raft of photographs. The housekeeper had no time perhaps to clean the silver frames. The oil painting over the mantel was of this same woman fifty years ago, beautiful as they all were then. The chairs were upholstered in velvet, there were fine ornaments. But there was something chill in the room, dust in the corners. *You can't get good help these days*. Almeida knew she was cast as the necessary stranger.

Mr. Speight looked smaller as his mother spoke.

"I'm easy to get on with. Harold is going to be away for two weeks, he says. Though with all this technology, he would be better off working here. When he moved his computer downstairs, it was in order that he needn't go away so often. My daughter, who might have come to stay, is in Mexico. For no good reason."

"What exactly would you want me to do?"

"I need company. Someone to read and talk and share my dinner. Stay overnight."

"Mother doesn't like to eat alone." Then he went on to answer her unasked question. "Mrs. Santos doesn't read well and goes home at four. She has a family."

"Do you have any special needs, Mrs. Kerwell?"

Special needs! As if she was the invalid!

"No," she said to Mrs. Speight who could be no more than ten years her senior and yet was very old. "Thank you." Her only special need was a way of getting out of this as fast as she could.

"It's important to know the value of fine things."

"I'm sure Mrs. Kerwell understands that." Harold sounded desperate.

"I see you have a Bernard Sly desk downstairs."

It was enough. Mrs. Speight and Harold smiled at her, same mouth, same teeth. She was in. Watching TV was not a waste of time.

"I'll be down in a moment," he said, dismissing her.

She walked downstairs and intended to march right out the door past the stone lions and on to the street but was in the middle of the drawing room before she knew it and back in the chair by the fireplace. The atmosphere was dark. Outside, snowflakes were falling. The streetlights had come on. In a moment, Mrs. Santos would enter and close the drapes.

With a long taper, the maid lights the candles in the piano brackets.

"He won't be long," she says although it's not her place to speak and no one knows exactly to whom she refers. The aunt is playing softly, Chopin perhaps. Frederick tells Adélie the truth about her mother.

"You will come to love me, Adélie. Good things do not happen in a day."

Adélie dreams of her home in the narrow street in Bruges. Her father has sent her here to marry this man, to support her three brothers. She is a beggar. But she is wearing silk.

A shot rings out. The screen is knocked over. A lick of flame catches it and spreads to the rug. Cries and screams. Running footsteps. Servants rush in with water. Soon horses hooves are heard outside. The fire truck. Bells ringing. The damage is confined to this room. The area round the fireplace has to be rebuilt.

They all know who is dead, and why.

Mr. Speight returned and sat behind the desk again. "Mother worries a little," he said, smiling now. "It's not always easy for me to get away. She does tend to get sudden spells. The doctor is attentive and will come very quickly if called. Now and then she forgets her medicine."

His eyes were like spaniel's eyes. Almeida wanted to offer him candy, to pat his head.

His phone rang and he spoke softly into it, looking apologetically at her, wanting sympathy for his busy life, his inherited possessions, his longing to escape.

The funeral is over.

Frederick is whispering, "You shall embroider another fire screen, Adélie. And I will always care for you."

The aunt talks to Frederick as if Adélie were deaf, "She'll get over it. It's been a shock. There is nothing like occupation. Buy her some more thread, another canvas. Work is a great cure."

"Will she ever speak again?"

"You'll be married in the garden."

Adélie hears those words and cries out, "No!"

"You see," the aunt says, "she does respond. All will be well."

"I do apologise," Mr. Speight said. "You may be wondering."

Almeida felt that she should perhaps, Jane Eyre-like,

respond by saying, *Oh sir, it's not my place to wonder.* But she did begin to wonder why she'd let herself be talked into this interview. On the phone, she had been told only that she would be a companion to an elderly woman. She reminded herself that she'd begun to dip into her savings for gifts for the grandchildren and had bought a new winter coat that would have to last the entire rest of her life.

"I hope you don't wear scent."

"Mrs. Speight has allergies?"

"I do. A great number of things bring on an attack."

The smell of pot pourri faded to an antiseptic reality.

"Mother isn't what you'd call sick," he said. "She gets lonely. She was used to a different way of life."

"It can't be easy," Almeida replied. She took a last look at the small oval firescreen. That particular lion was ferocious, its mouth was open wide, snarling; there was a hint of blood, one paw was raised to strike.

"My great-grandmother embroidered that screen," he said.

"She never did get back to Europe, did she?"

He looked at her strangely and said, "Those are old stories. But you will come?"

"I don't think I'm quite right for you," she replied. "You need someone younger."

"But no. You're exactly the kind of person. It's only a few evenings. I can be back in ten days if I have to, eleven at most. Please."

As she went out of the door, Almeida turned and looked past him at the lion's head umbrella stand and beyond it at the ghost of the woman who had never gone to Africa.

"Take time," he said. "Perhaps when you've thought it over. Call me tomorrow."

"You have a lovely home," she replied.

"Mother took to you."

Big of her, Almeida thought but said, "How kind," and knew it was no better.

In the middle of the street she stopped and looked to either side at the mansions set solidly in their quarter acres as if they wanted with their brick and stone to press nature back, to weight it down and always keep it in its place.

Hey cut this out, she said to herself. *Back off.* She'd reverted to her late teens when it was burn the rich or at least make them share or failing that, suffer.

Fourteen evenings. Five in the evening till ten in the morning. Was it too much to give to an older woman whose life had been constrained? To a woman whose daughter was in Mexico and didn't seem eager to return? Yes, in fact, at this moment in her own life, it was.

She turned too sharply to walk on and felt the pain in her leg, sharper than usual, persistent. There was no way she could get to the subway. She limped back to the house. Mrs. Santos would have to call a taxi for her.

She climbed up the stone steps again. They might as well have been the side of a mountain for the effort it took. She pressed the bell and put her arm round the nearest lion for support.

As she slid to the ground, Harold Speight opened the door. He looked down at her and said, "I knew you'd come back, Mrs. Kerwell."

Another Story

"I knew at the time what he was doing was dangerous," Jess said.

Almeida had read all the books she ever wanted to read. On TV, disasters abounded and Harriet was no longer there to help the earthquake victims, the distraught, the dispossessed. Melvin had found maturity at fifty. Sharon and Tyler spoke a foreign language. Geraldine went from house to hospital to office to house, competent, cheerful, in her element. There was no reason to get out of this neat white bed ever again. She could lie here in an aura of no-name cologne and disinfectant till the sound was turned off and the picture faded to black.

Jean had moved to Huntsville and was talking of moving even further away. She'd left a hole in her friend's life so large that a herd of elephants could have fallen into it. Lunch with other women only underlined Jean's absence. Helen kept pressing her to join the bridge group and Annie wasn't much interested in life beyond her own family.

"Come and stay," Jean wrote. "You'll love it here. We'll look after you. Bill makes a great omelette." *I miss you,* was there between the lines but there was no apology, nothing to suggest she was aware she had left her friend of forty years in the lurch. It was Jean who should be sitting here beside her instead of this vision of mutton done up as young art student.

"I knew at the time what he was doing was dangerous," Jess said again.

"It was nothing. Nothing happened."

"How can you say that! What did you know? You were ten years old. You've always done this. Turned your head away from real things."

"The war left him strange. He came to see me later. He used to pick me up and drive me to work. In that big car."

"I'm talking about my father for Chrissake. The way he was holding his gun."

Almeida's mouth dried. They hadn't talked about the accident for fifty years and she wasn't sure why they should now except that she was a captive and had no choice but to listen. A pillow over her face might be kinder than to dredge up the old story.

She picked at the gift of grapes. They looked at each other across the silence and saw a bullet wound, a shattered leg bone, a lake of tears.

Jess, recalling maybe that she was there to comfort and cheer, only said, "Well it sure changed my life."

[186]

"What were you looking for that day?"

"You know how he loved venison."

A feast was spread out before them on a stiff white cloth. Mother was carving meat she'd never liked, serving it with red cabbage, juniper berry sauce, scalloped potatoes. It was Thanksgiving. It was Christmas. It was Easter. It was long ago.

"Mom liked a colourful table."

The beige remains on the hospital tray were of doubtful stew and rice pudding.

"I know it was dangerous. The whole thing was dangerous. But what?"

"Suddenly moving like that with a loaded gun in his hand."

A wood, firs, birches, the smell of wet leaves, the faint sound of a stream under ice, the stillness of apprehension. Weeds with wiry stalks waiting to trip a man. The animals' revenge.

"It was carelessness."

"Aren't most accidents?"

A young orderly came in and picked up the tray. At the door she remembered she'd been told to interact with the patients.

"Did you enjoy your dinner, Mrs Kerwell?" she asked and was smart enough to dodge away without waiting for the answer.

Apropos of nothing, Jess said, "I've got to go and buy my lottery tickets."

"Do you ever win?"

"I used to think I'd be the millionth. You know. To walk into a store or up to an airport counter to get my boarding pass and have a person come to me and say, you are our millionth customer. Balloons would fall from the sky and there'd be cheers, champagne, a big cheque, free rides forever. Like fame for a minute, eh Almy?"

"When you were a kid you believed in magic."

"Chasing rainbows. The gold was there. I was in the wrong place, that's all."

Almeida found the strength to ask, "And now?"

Before Jess had come into the room, she'd been lying there figuring how many four-letter words you could make out of *continent*. A word which could mean a large land mass, the ability to hold on, to control, chaste. But put *i* and *n* in front of it and it becomes a joke, a nightmare of a joke.

If they would only all leave her alone, she could invent another world and move into it, people it with slim, well-dressed men and women who lived in harmony and spoke with poetic intelligence. But the nurse kept making her get out of bed. Mona had glided by last night, radiant, newly in love, still grateful, still not saying which of Almeida's words had restored her to normality. Through a haze, she recalled Helen appearing and leaving on her bedside table a copy of *Bridge for Beginners*. The physiotherapist demanded impossible contortions while Almeida whimpered that the operation was only the day before yesterday. Martha had appeared early this morning. Or was it an illusion that her cousin had bent over her telling her she would be up and about much quicker if she took this magic potion?

But here in the flesh was Jess saying in all but words, *now you know what it feels like.*

She had no choice but to entertain these actors who

appeared before her, said their lines, practised pitying looks, and made their exits. *Go on, go back to your little lives*, she wanted to shout after them. She could hear them murmuring as they walked down the corridor, *Poor Almeida*.

She gritted her teeth and said to her sister, "Nice of you to come. What are you working on now?"

"I'm trying to make sense of things. I've time now. Particularly that day."

That day when Dad cried his eyes out. Never cheerful again so it seemed. Mother calm, making that huge effort to pretend all would be well and that a girl with a limp would have no problems in life, in love, in having children. Getting Almeida to give up her cherished rabbit, telling her to be kind. *Take this to your sister. Play with Jess.* And in return Jess had painted her favourite dolls black.

"I've nearly got it figured," Jess said.

"He wasn't a careful man."

"That day in the meadow."

"You were in a forest."

"I'm talking about Uncle George."

"He wasn't there."

"That day when I ran on and on and you came back and there was a fuss. What happened? I felt guilty. I should've stayed."

"It didn't matter." Almeida withdrew into an invalid's justifiable weariness. The conversation had shifted in midstream and she wanted to think of pleasing colours, of blue and green and a boat drifting down a river.

Through half-closed eyes, she looked at her sister. Jess was wearing a loose top in purples and reds and yellows.

Her hair was thin now, too often dyed red or gold. Colour had always beaten out style in her wardrobe. She was pulling on a leather jacket that was rubbed at the edges and missing a button. She caught Almeida's thought in mid-air.

Softly, gently, because she was talking to a woman in pain, she said, "I would've liked it if you'd said, once, something like, You've got to have a new jacket to wear. I'll buy you that blue one you liked. Or, your hair needs shaping, I'll take you to my man, or woman."

"My life hasn't been what you've thought."

"I've watched your life."

"I've stood back." Almeida could hear herself using words that were Harriet's. "I've respected your space. I thought you were living the way you wanted."

"Shouting isn't a bad thing. I've discovered that."

Almeida's tongue wouldn't get round the words, *Harriet loved you.* She couldn't, right now, give her sister that gift. On the next visit she would make the effort. It was owed to her.

"Who's the big bouquet from?"

"Oh. The man whose house I fell in front of."

Mr Speight, perhaps fearing a court case, had been the first to make an appearance on this cramped stage. He had entered diffidently behind a cover of carnations and roses and green boughs. In that scene he was cast as suppliant rather than would-be employer. "I've put off my trip," he'd said. "Perhaps when you're better. You wouldn't need to walk much." "There are lots of women in town who'd do this for you." "You just seem exactly right to us, Mrs Kerwell." *Goodbye and thank you, Harold.*

"I brought you this, " Jess said.

Almeida took the package and began to unwrap it slowly. It was flat. It had corners. It was an inch and a half thick and measured about ten by twelve. At first glance, the picture looked like an abstract in shades of brown and white.

"I was working in oils then."

The shapes resolved into a tree without a trunk, the severed top holding up its branches in tribute towards soft rounded clouds. In the centre, a figure in a dress was running through the sky.

"It's—good."

"It's what I could see from my hospital window. Imprinted on my mind. The day they told me my leg would never be quite all right. I've never been able to put it on the wall. I thought you might like it now."

"Thank you."

"I think what's always bothered me is I could have jumped out of the way."

"He fell back."

"That's what we said. Both of us."

Almeida looked at the painting again. She tried to see beyond the image.

"Dad always knew what he was doing."

"Don't say that, Jess."

"Have you been jealous of me, Almy?"

"You were, you seemed, free."

"Free to be lonely, free to be short of cash, free to wear odd shoes, pantihose with one leg wrinkled."

"But you have—done things. You have expressed yourself."

"A person always suffers for that, one way or another."

"Yes, it was dangerous."

"He found it hard to smile at me after, my Dad."

"He found it hard to smile period."

"When did we lose sight of each other, Almeida?"

"Dad didn't think much of me because I wouldn't learn to shoot."

"It was because you weren't his."

"Jess!"

Almeida raised herself too far off the bed and cried out in pain.

"Uncle George was your Dad. He had an affair with Mom. You knew, surely. I mean, look at you."

Jess pulled a handmirror out of her purse and thrust it at her. Almeida saw an old man, the old man from the bus, and the real old man who had driven her to town so silently, the man who had sat there at her graduation, crying.

"Is this what you wanted to do?" Almeida yelled. "Come in here when I'm helpless, when Joe's lying there. And tell me lies."

"You knew. You must have known. Everybody else did."

"Get out. Go away. Leave me alone."

"I'm sorry. But you must've known."

"GET OUT!"

Jess was gone. Half sister or whole. All of her gone and her ridiculous story with her.

Almeida lay back in the bed. Tiredness fell over her like a too-heavy blanket. She could hear her only re-

[192]

maining daughter down the corridor talking to the nurse. Geraldine would see her aunt and run to her and hug her. They would talk about her and there was no way she could get out of bed and defend herself. She lay back on the pillow and heard the door open and close. Thinking her asleep, Jess and Geraldine would go together to see Joe and murmur to him, hoping that through his stricken mind, he could understand. *Almeida is doing well,* they would say. *She misses you. You're looking good today.*

They wouldn't say, *And she regrets the two years she spent apart from you. She feels guilty. It was lost time. She always loved you.*

She turned again to the painting. It seemed a cruel gift. To remind her that now she too was no longer whole, not perfect. And like her sister, she had to come to terms with being lame at least for a time. And then as she looked more closely, she saw that the figure in the painting, the girl running through the clouds, was wearing a dress the colour of ripe lemons.

Jessica! Sister! Almeida tried to call out. So much for the extra insurance for a private room. There was no one to help when she needed it. She pressed the button by her bed but what was she to tell the nurse? *Fetch my sister back to me. At once. I have to talk to her.*

So everybody knew, did they! Everybody! Mother, Geraldine, Harriet, Sharon, Tyler, Star and Sapphire, the entire world including Jean's son Dwayne, the mailman, the man on the Sea Wall in Vancouver. And all this time, Jess had been thinking, saying, that she was their Dad's only child.

Almeida began to move her good left leg to one side and then up and down. She could hop. Pirates with wooden legs got around fast enough. She had to get after that woman and when she caught up with her she would shout out.

JESS! Just you listen to me. My father was the man who took me to school on the first day, who took a picture of me at graduation and had it enlarged to poster size. He was the man who was there at breakfast time and dinner time, who bought my shoes. Who cried and laughed at my wedding. That's who my father was. You can't take him away from me, Jess.

Enter briskly a woman who looked as though she cycled fifty kilometres to work every day and lifted sacks of cement for pleasure.

"Exercise time, " she said. "Let's get moving, Almeida. We need your space."

In spite of the pain and some dread of detaching her new hip joint, Almeida managed to raise her right leg half an inch off the bed. The fight wasn't over. Not while she had breath.

Home Invasion

Something was eating the house. It was nine-thirty in the morning and life was full of uncertainty. Almeida and the cat eyed each other.

" Just do the job you're hired to do," she said to it, "and I'll see you're fed. Otherwise you'll be out there in the rain dodging the heavy traffic."

"Mother!" Geraldine had let herself in and was standing by the door, taking off her raincoat, shaking the drips onto the mat.

"I don't think it can understand."

"They do."

"Well not this one. It has a dumb look to it."

The cat stalked off towards the living room no doubt to dig its claws into the furniture.

"I've brought you a loaf and milk and six cans of cat food. Esther said he likes the liver best."

The house didn't even smell like hers any more. Tyler in a five-year-old's chirp had once said that Grandma's house smelled of cake and trees. Today she was conscious of an air of decay; old, used breath with a hint of fresh cat. It wasn't that she wanted to dance round the rooms naked or hang upside down from the curtain rail but a person should have privacy, should be able to do whatever weird thing she wanted when her door was locked.

"You should call before you come."

"I was passing. I'm showing a house on Brenton."

"I could be out," Almeida said and realised that it made no difference. Humans with keys, like mice, could come and go whether she was there or not. "Have you time for coffee?"

Gerry had become the responsible child, Almeida the responsibility. Neither of them was entirely comfortable with the arrangement. But in any case, comfort had left the house when Almeida found scraps of wood and plaster on the floor in the corner. She'd taken the books off the shelves and put them on the table. They were her old friends and she didn't want to see them chewed. MacDonald, Buchan, Dietrich, Emily Carr, Hepburn, Tracy. She had tracked other lives for years before moving on to the library's True Crime selection.

She'd kept Joe's accounts of this battle or that, stories of heroes and the 'real' war that he felt he'd missed by being on the ground collecting data instead of up in the sky, flying a plane. Time and again he'd said to her, as if he wanted her to see a more important truth, *You should read this, Almy.*

Some people read to supply what their own lives lack, like adding vitamins to food. Gerry preferred romantic novels. Harriet had loved Dumas and James Bond and Scott until she'd found her own great adventures. And Jean used to wander in other worlds; life on Mars, creatures in space. But what was Jean reading now, re-married and re-moved to the warm West coast? Recipe books?

"Mom, you were miles away?"

"What does Melvin read?"

"You know what he likes, sports magazines, financial self-help stuff. The other day though, I found a book of poems on his bedside table."

Poems? Melvin! If he hadn't in the past two years become a reformed, better Melvin, Almeida would at once have suspected him of cheating on her daughter. When a man of plain speech turns to flights of fancy, he might as well take to wearing his coat inside out. Almeida refrained from asking if there were lipstick stains on his collar.

Gerry was at the counter filling the kettle, examining the cord, the plug.

"We have to get you one that turns itself off."

"I'm not senile."

Yet hung in the air, a mocking clown of a word.

Even The Voice next door had got in on the act. Last week she'd said in that wall-piercing tone, "I'll keep an eye on her, Geraldine," leaving Almeida wincing and feeling like a silly child who couldn't be trusted. She was not prepared to be old and fragile. *This side up. With care!* Even young people fell down in the street for Crissake.

"Melvin says he'll come and fix your dryer at the weekend."

[197]

Oh give him a key too. Give the kids one each. And Jess. No not Jess. But Martha. Why not? Hand them out at the subway station!

But gratitude was called for here. She smiled and said thank you and offered her daughter a slice of the lemon cake she'd baked the day before.

"No thanks, Mom. No use me going to the gym and working out and then eating cake in the morning."

Gerry had become stream-lined. She moved quickly. Her cell phone hardly had a chance to cool down. Two years in a row she'd made salesperson of the year and was aiming for three. And what was this top salesperson doing now if not casting her eyes over the walls, checking out the floor space?

"How much?" Almeida said sharply.

"Two hundred and fifty K," Geraldine answered and then blushed. "Sorry, Mom. I can't help it."

There'll come a time. The words unsaid. The move to a place with no stairs. *Do you want to keep all these ornaments? We'll come and see you every week, mother. You'll be comfortable here.* Sound of a clanging gate.

"You and Dad kept it in good shape."

"We lived here forty years. Aside from that little break I had. I'm fine dear, you know. There's no need to be doing this every day. My hip's nearly like new. I could dance if I wanted."

"It's no trouble, Mom. Till you get used to Dawson."

There was a proverb. Granddad had said it was Russian. *There's lots of ways to skin a cat but no way the cat's going to like it.* Here and now Almeida felt more like the skinned than the skinner but she couldn't have said exactly why.

[198]

"Your great-granddad used to say everything he didn't like, or that was violent, was Russian. But you have to remember, he lived in those times."

Gerry looked at her watch.

"Mustn't keep my buyer waiting."

"I hope you sell it, dear."

"She's desperate to get something in that area."

Desperate! Desperate was something Harriet had seen firsthand. Harriet had known what *desperate* meant. And it had nothing at all to do with having enough money to buy a residence in a desirable area with five bedrooms and a sunken marble tub.

"That's where the Speights lived, on Brenton."

"It's their house. Been on the market for months. Since the old lady died. There's a daughter. She's sorted everything out."

"What happened to him?"

"Walked out of the house after her funeral, straight to Las Vegas."

"You sure it wasn't Africa?"

"There was a woman in Vegas."

As she went out, Gerry said, "Don't worry. If it's mice, he'll soon get rid of them for you."

She called out to the cat, "Mom will learn to love you, Dawson," and closed the door.

Almeida had tried to think of the mice as small furry creatures as much entitled to their share of the house as she was, but Granddad's word for such pests was varmints. They were varmints to him and they were varmints to her. The cat, a larger varmint, returned to the kitchen and was staring at her again. Killer, companion, spy.

[199]

"I am not my own woman any more," she said to it. And stopped still.

Because each of those separate words struck her mind like a clapper hitting the side of a bell. They echoed in her head, filling it with sound and crashing from one side to another. She sat down in Joe's chair and the cries of a thousand Saturday nights came from the box in the corner. *He shoots. It hits the goalposts. He's down. My God did you see that. Shall we go to a movie? They're playing the Canucks. There's a party at the Schroeder's. It's the play-offs. You go, sweetheart.*

Seven years old, seventeen, twenty-seven. When had she owned her own time, her own body, her comings and goings.

Look after Jess. She needs you now.

I have to get home. Joe will be back.

I must get back, the kids will be home.

And what did Geraldine say to her friends now or to Melvin? *I have to go. I need to see that Mom's all right. She's alone now.*

She belonged to her daughter just as her daughters had once belonged to her.

For two years, before the trip to China, she'd created a kind of freedom. A space she'd made her own and enjoyed. But Harriet's death had come to remind her that she'd gained nothing by that move.

And then Joe too had left without a word. Slowly, silently, those last months, he'd made his escape. At the service, the minister had said that they were together now, father and daughter. Most likely he thought that was a useful thing to say. She'd held back from telling him he was an idiot. Though she did, willy-nilly, find herself looking upwards whenever she thought about Joe or Harriet, as if there was a heaven and they were sitting around in it chatting pleasantly with a host of new friends.

"When was I ever my own woman?" she shouted towards the ceiling. "Tell me that!" She waited a moment. There was no reply.

The pile of letters and cards was gathering dust, six months' dust, and yellowing at the edges, in a basket on the table. Kindly words of sympathy. Offers of care and love, *thinking of you at this sad time.* Time to get rid of them or put them away upstairs with those others, the ones she could still hardly bear to read. She picked out Jean's long letter. *You'd really like it here, Almy. The trees are in bloom. You can walk nearly every day. You should give it a try, a month or two. There's a town house....*

I miss you, was there unsaid. But it was three thousand miles away. A truly impossible distance. She had no seven-league boots. She picked up the basket. Halfway up the stairs, she heard a noise. Footsteps heavier than any rodent's. A shadow moved across the hall. *I've gone out of my mind. I'm seeing figments. This is all I need now, a house full of wandering ghosts. I will throw myself down the stairs.* But this figment had a voice.

It said, "How're you doing, Almeida?"

"How did you get in?"

"Gerry left the door open."

So it was a conspiracy. *Speak to her. It was a bit of a shock at the funeral but she'll get over it.*

Jess was holding a cup of coffee and biting into a piece of cake. A varmint too big for Dawson to get his teeth round.

"What do you want?"

"I'm your sister."

"What does that mean?"

"I'm sorry. What I said. I suppose."

"What?"

"I suppose it was because you were lying there."

"Helpless."

"I knew what it felt like."

"That usually makes people kind."

Almeida couldn't stand it. They were coming at her from all sides. Opening her door, walking in, sitting in her chairs uninvited, picking up crumbs. She threw the basket of letters down the stairs, they floated and fluttered and she hobbled down after them. Even in her anger, her new hip reminded her that she would soon have to move to a level place, a neat all-on-one-floor space.

"I won't have people coming in here whenever they like," she shouted.

Jess ran into the kitchen and began to cry.

"And crying and laughing or any other goddam thing. This is my house. It is not a café. Not a public place. And it is not a stage either."

"All right, "Jess said. "I'm going. I won't be back. You can get old and die on your own if you want. I only wanted to say that I didn't mean what I said, about Dad."

"I know he was my father."

"I'm not talking about that. It really was an accident. When he shot me. Just some days, I've thought he kind of meant it. Some days I've wanted to think that. I don't suppose you can understand. It made it easier to think that. Accidents are so fucking unforgivable."

She picked up her purse and began to walk out very

slowly. Almeida wanted to call her back and tell her she was right, accidents are unforgivable, no one knew that more than she did. But her throat had closed. She couldn't cry out either that her sister had no right to bring that young man to Joe's funeral, both of them dressed in outrageous colours. She couldn't yell out that she was sorry for Jess's damaged life. That she knew she could have done more to help. She watched through the window as Jess went down the front path, limping more than she used to. She sent a message to her brain to raise her arm so she could knock on the window and beckon Jess back to the house. But her arm stayed by her side. The message was delayed.

She locked the door and put the chain on. Jess would tell Gerry that her mother had shouted out, had been hysterical, hostile. Gerry would come round with soothing words and possibly drugs.

She turned on the radio and bent to pick up the letters. Her hip let her know it wasn't ready for aerobics yet. The radio voice said she had a chance to win a trip for two to Hawaii. Just call this number. Answer this question.

She poured herself a cup of coffee and sat down. With all these visitors she was going to need a bigger coffee maker. Eight cup? Ten cup? Industrial size?

"My life is everyone else's," she said to Dawson.

The cat leapt on to her lap and reached up and patted her face in a way it probably thought was charming. She set it down on the floor.

"No," she said. "I'm going to buy traps."

If she kept the beast, in no time she'd be saying to Helen, to Annie, *I have to get back home, Pussy needs feed-*

ing. I can't come and help out at the shelter today. I have to take Pussy to the vet. She saw the cat attached to the other end of a string, tied to the house, tied to her.

"There are nice people out there who would call you snookums and give you salmon and cream."

It appeared to listen.

"Maybe I can't turn somersaults but I can move. I love my daughter but she has a life, she has two lives. For ten years, fifteen years, she will come every day and look after me and she'll get old doing it. I will take up her time. Prime of life time. She shouldn't have to do this. She'll come to resent Harriet for not staying around to share the burden.

"I'm not kidding you for a minute, Dawson, with all this sob stuff, am I? Making it look like self-sacrifice. What we're talking about here is self-preservation. Right. Yours and mine."

Jean had spoken to her of the joys of life near the sea, such a change from Huntsville and the city. She was a volunteer at the hospital. She helped buy groceries for the housebound. It needn't be an idle withdrawal. And there was bowling. Bowling! Jean and Bill spent a lot of time on a square of green hurling large balls after a smaller one.

But they could be neighbours again. Have lunch every Saturday. And there would be time to tell Jean she was putting too much oatmeal in those cookies. Sharon and Tyler would come and visit. They could go kayaking and stay at her house and she would make blueberry pies. Gerry and Mel would make it their winter getaway place. And maybe next Spring, she would invite Jess and they would sit there over coffee, two older women letting their bad memories fade, learning to kiss and make up. And since it was her place, she would always get to have the last word.

"I can't shovel the snow any more, cat. There's that to think of too. I'll be a prisoner here after a storm till some kind person comes and sets me free. And who needs ice at my age. I used to love ice. Me and Jess too, before her accident, skating on the pond. I'd be out there till it was getting dark and I'd been called in for the sixth time."

"ALMEIDA!"

She hadn't locked the back door. This intruder appeared from the kitchen. Smiling, her slight figure belying the hefty voice, she said, "I've made barley soup. Want to come over for lunch?"

The kindness trap. Could she say at 11.30 that she'd eaten lunch already? Or would that lead to a phone call to Gerry to say, your mother's eating her meals at strange times? And then people possibly older than she was would be delivering hot dinners to her door.

Quickly she said, "Thank you, Debbie, that's kind of you. But I'm having lunch with a friend."

"Well if you're sure."

If you're sure! As if she wouldn't know one day from another. She smiled at her neighbour and didn't ask her to sit down but moved quickly as though she was getting ready to go downtown. Debbie looked at her doubtfully and backed out with the dire words, "Have a good lunch. I'll look in on you later."

Confusion rained down, scrappy thoughts. Why were they doing this? She was in decent health. Other people her age were still working. She managed to walk now with one cane and didn't always need that. Had she become a necessary care-object for her family, for her lonely neighbour, for a goddam cat?

There was a scrabbling noise in the cupboard under the sink. Dawson ignored it.

But her life was reduced to this, to a cat and a key. A cat and a door that was never quite closed. A neighbour popping in to check that she hadn't let the bath run over, boiled the saucepan dry, put her clothes on backwards. A daughter whose duty it was to look in on her each day and see she was all right.

The cat meowed. It was hungry. It looked at her with those deep green eyes. Colours of black and orange and white swirled on its coat to make pleasing pattern. He was a handsome creature who deserved a better home.

"Don't look at me like that, Dawson. You think I'm an ungrateful bitch. Right. You're telling me millions of older folk would love to have all this attention."

I'm talking to a cat, Joe. Now I'm talking to you and you're gone.

On the radio. The end of an old song. Joe had liked it and sometimes tried to imitate that melancholy voice singing, *Chances are.* The song played out. "The weather today for Toronto. Cloudy with showers. Chance of snow later. And now for the news."

She turned the knob and stopped a recitation of the day's tragedies: grey ships gathering in the Gulf a second time, politicians arguing over Quebec. They had their problems. She had hers. She walked up and down, measured the room, looked at the walls with Gerry's eyes. The dining area needed a new coat of paint. Threadbare was the word for the living-room rug.

If I'm not careful, I could soon be an elderly woman sitting alone in one room, a room with beige walls.

Chances are. Chance of snow. Chance'd be a fine thing. Chances are I could step on to the street and be hit by a passing bus. Chances are I could win the lottery. But only if I buy a ticket. And that's a matter of choice.

"The thing is, Dawson, you can't choose who owns you," she said. "But I sure as hell can."

She dialled the distant number and heard the ring, saw Jean moving towards the phone, saw Bill's querying look, saw leafy trees outside the windows. Could she manage the long journey? Would Geraldine feel betrayed? No one answered. They were out. It was over. She wouldn't call again. The brave moment, the chance, had gone. And the 'in' was gone from independence. Her door was open. Debbie and Dawson and Gerry were her kindly keepers.

Then she heard her old friend's voice, breathless, saying, "Just got in."

"Is that place next door to you still for rent?" Almeida asked.

And the cat, as if it understood every word, padded over to the door and sat down to wait.